SCENT *of a* TRUFFLE

Mischief and Legacy in the Dordogne Valley

Cécile Ganne

Cover Design and Typesetting: Covered by Kerry LLC

ISBN (Paperback): 979-8-9909818-0-5

ISBN (Hardcover): 979-8-9909818-2-9

ISBN (Ebook): 979-8-9909818-1-2

UN GRAND MERCI

I want to thank my family for their loving support, my husband and friends for their many keen insights and suggestions. And, most especially, my big brother for his commitment, creativity, and his infectious enthusiasm and optimism during this meandering journey over the last two decades.

To my boys.

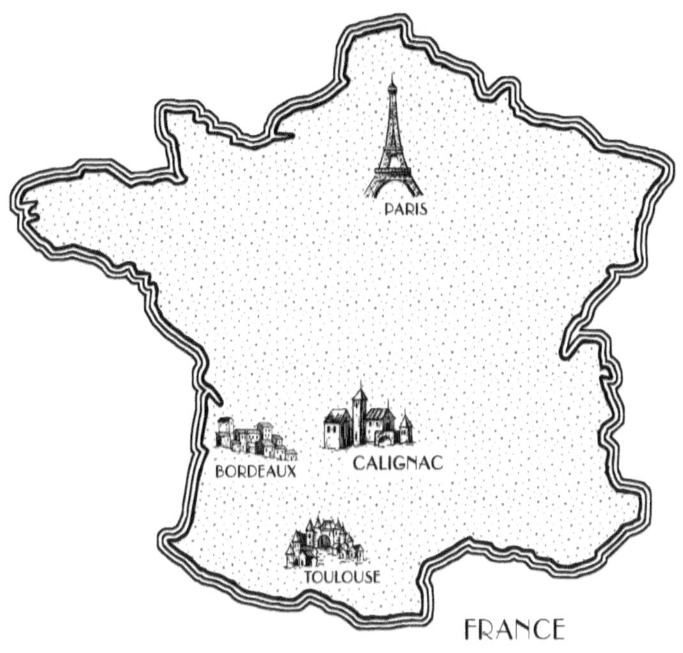

Steeped in history and culture, the region of *Quercy* stretches north of Toulouse and east of Bordeaux, encompassing much of the southwestern French *départements* of Lot and Tarn-et-Garonne.

Amidst this landscape lies Calignac, the fictional medieval village at the heart of our tale. Tucked away east of the Dordogne River, this place of wonder is renowned for its walnuts, wine, and black truffles.

CONTENTS

FOREWORD

The stories we tell ourselves always have the last word.
This one is birthed in my childhood memories of south-west France.
Waves of smells, tastes, and textures abound.
Village markets exploding with colors, aromas, and impassioned exchanges.
Red ribbons of tilled earth glistening against the white limestone cliffs in the distance.
Dipping flights of swallows on summer eves when the dry smell of coumarin rises from the Dordogne Valley.
The tall poplars along the river, still to this day, haunt my imagination—their dark shadows etched deeply into the lineaments and intonations of my psyche.
I grew up in a small village where life, "back then," seemed simple.
Ancestral rituals. Generous ideals. Mysterious serenity.

The passage of time magically magnifying memories? Possibly!

Still, there must have been something as these formative influences have endured the vagaries of life.

They have been the underpinning of how I decided to bring up my kids and dedicate my life to painting and teaching.

Writing this novella has allowed me to reconnect with my affirming self—the enduring refuge for the soul, no matter what.

Like a sacred past that needed to be channeled, told, and celebrated.

A pondering on upbringing. A reaffirming of my roots. An ode to life.

I hope this book inspires you to do the same.

CHAPTER ONE

Tucked against towering limestone cliffs, the French village of Calignac overlooked the lush corn fields of the Dordogne Valley. A few miles to the south, its river meandered nonchalantly between tall poplars and strands of pebbly beaches. On sunny days, it glistened dreamingly; on rainy days, it hid under a wide vaporous veil.

Ever since the feats and miracles of Saint Calin centuries ago, Calignac seemed a delectable and dreamy land, a place where tradition and secrecy lingered in the whispers of the villagers and the shadows of ancient oak trees. Each season, all were poised towards the celebration of the Truffle Fair showcasing its local fungus, the most prodigious and rarest black truffle.

Calignac seemed impervious to the passing of time. Its houses clustered like mushrooms around the charming Romanesque church. In typical southern French architectural style, each house rested on thick century-old stone walls topped with perfectly lined gray-blue slate roofs.

Pilgrims still passed through the village on their way to the renowned pilgrimage of St. James in northern Spain. They walked along the same narrow wall sheltered paths that had existed for centuries. Creasing the countryside like the bark of a tree through pristine woods of oaks, the network of paths—or cow paths as locals affectionately called them—remained the shepherds' coveted routes when shifting their cattle from field to field.

It was precisely the poetry of this deeply furrowed landscape that had caught St. Calin's imagination when he decided to settle there in the Middle Ages. A Franciscan monk, he had dedicated his life to alleviating the suffering of others by concocting special ointments made with herbs from the local woods. The mystery of his healing powers had left an imprint on villagers' minds, for as children, they all remembered listening to the tales of his feats and miraculous cures.

Among St. Calin's many legacies was the village fountain that he had carved from local limestone. An underground spring, the origins of which remain unknown to this day, flowed nonchalantly and inexhaustibly in its center, even in the worst of droughts. Medieval archives recorded its mysterious properties: it had cured great ills and infections, washing them away as if making stains magically disappear.

At the pinnacle of the fountain, stood the wiry figure of St. Calin, cast in worn bronze, as a timeless sentinel, forever in the guise of a humble pilgrim. His eyes, carved with the tender wisdom of the ages, seemed to reach all corners of the square, reminding villagers of his eternal sagacity and blessed permanence.

One summer morning, Trouvert, who had been Calignac's priest for fifty years, was surveying the square as he left the sacristy to get fresh flowers for the altar. Fridays were his favorite day of the week when Calignac bustled with energy. The church required regular cleaning. Luckily, he could rely on the devout and kind-hearted Madame Sardelois to keep the nave and transept spotless.

He scanned the lavish vegetable and flower stalls that wrapped around the church. Blessed was the soil of the Dordogne Valley, abounding with sediment so rich that asparagus shot up like weeds. At this time of year, fruits were also abundant. Delicious apples and tart pomegranates; curvaceous purple figs; golden freckled *Mirabelle* plums and voluptuous *pêches de vigne* covered with soft, fragrant fuzz.

The August breeze was filled with dried tobacco leaves, roasted chicken, *duck confits,* and the sweet scent of warm bread wafting from the *Boulangerie,* the local bakery. Further along, velvety mounds of small soft cheeses battled against a backdrop of imposing wheels and delectable wedges of firmer cheeses.

Trouvert walked briskly despite being in his eighties.

He was thinking about the next celebration to organize in honor of the Saint's anniversary. He planned to lead his parishioners into a festive procession from the fountain down to the river; always a good way to prompt them to reflect on their connections to their patron.

He stopped at the local café, on the other side of the marketplace. Under the large pergola, laden with rambunctious wisteria seemingly in endless bloom, he shared a coffee with several villagers and listened to their news. Even those who never came for confession readily shared their troubles or asked for his advice. His kind blue eyes told the story of a man who had humbly dedicated his life to meeting villagers in the fields, on the roads, or wherever they needed him. In fact, his tall and evanescent figure wrapped in his dark cassock was often seen billowing in the distance. Life was a complicated nexus of experiences and decisions, and he understood that when the narrow path was challenging, courage and fortitude went a long way.

On the other side of the marketplace, Debasse, the town mayor, strutted through the loud crowd like a monarch. Now well into his forties, he saw the marketplace as a stage to flaunt his power and measure his influence. He had little knowledge or interest in mundane agricultural matters and cringed at the tiresome whingeing over the lack of rain or excess of sun. But he subjected himself to these trivial conversations and to the shaking of hands to rally enough votes for his most ambitious political proposals—not to mention his re-election.

And if his electors *thought* him a great and compassionate leader, then he *was*.

Debasse approached the *Bouchère's* stand. Screaming at the top of her lungs, the butcher's wife advertised her rows of mouth-watering *pâtés*, *rillettes*, and *saucissons*—*saucissons aux herbes* coated with fennel, rosemary, and thyme, or her specialty, *saucissons* sweetened with local saffron. Debasse was a *bon vivant* and well-known for his gargantuan and carnivorous appetites and scrumptious dinners. He intended on asking the *Bouchère* to set aside an exceptional piece of wild boar that caught his eye.

He paused to contemplate St. Calin's fountain where, at the end of summer, he proudly rang the brass bell to sound off the ninety-day countdown to the most anticipated fair in the southwest of France. Calignac's *Fête de la Truffe*, the famous Truffle Fair, captivated an entire region, attracting throngs of passionate connoisseurs hoping to discover this year's most delicately fragranced underground fungus, considered the region's black gold.

Besides his well-known healing powers, St. Calin was also thought to bring luck to truffle seekers—so much so that harvesting after St Calin's day was thought to be a harbinger of bad luck. Historically, the event culminated with the truffle contest; the best specimen won the blue ribbon, the most coveted distinction known on the gourmand's truffle map. Debasse now regarded the *Fête de la Truffe* as *his* moment of glory to shine as the consummate leader he believed himself to be.

Later that afternoon, after a copious lunch of

pheasant and chestnuts, Debasse started forth with bold energy. Past the cemetery, he took a right turn up the hill and headed towards Adèle's house. Debasse's wide cheeks contrasted with his sunken, prying eyes and large fleshy hands; they told the story of the insatiable hunger for money and social status which consumed his entire soul. Originally from a family of shady merchants, he had spent his youth in unscrupulous activities. Thankfully, his marriage a few decades back to the lovely Constance d'Aroux de La Serre, a descendant of one of the noblest families of the *Quercy* region, had restored his once-dubious reputation.

Debasse had been busy promoting his new motion, the one he desperately wanted to pass at the next municipal council. The vote was just a few weeks away. So far, the winds had been favorable to him, and many notables had given their support. Still, he needed one more vote—that of Adèle.

No one really knew her age; it seemed as though Adèle Montfort had always been a figurehead of Calignac. She was well-respected for her caring and sound wisdom; in fact, no one could recall a single instance when she had spared any effort to help others in need. Her kind heart was further strengthened by her love of tradition—a fondness that stemmed not from a tedious and blind respect for the past, but rather, from a genuine belief that ritual has the power to root the soul. For her, humans needed bearings to know where they came from, and thus, where they were going. She never disapproved of innovations, provided they served the soul of the community. Throughout her life, many had sought her advice, confident that she had their best interests at heart.

But Debasse was aware that Adèle had not always seen eye to eye with him over the years. He knew he could not underestimate her shrewdness and incisiveness. As he reached the hill, slightly out of breath, he paused and rested for a short while. At the end of two rows of sycamores stood Adèle's house, an elegant yet strong stone building that stood clutching the ground in the midst of the surrounding boxwoods. He walked through the wrought iron gate, across the crunchy gravel lane, and climbed the worn front steps. After obsessively checking the knot of his navy tie, he stared down at his shiny leather shoes and reached for the pewter bell.

CHAPTER TWO

Debasse stood waiting for a few minutes, stretching his back, which often bothered him at night. His wife said he needed to take more frequent walks for daily exercise, but he never listened, especially when he was fixated on more important matters. He heard some muffled footsteps. The latch released and the door opened in a warm breath onto a golden hallway of gleaming floors.

With a large canvas apron strapped across her corpulent chest, Bernardine welcomed him with swift gestures that concealed the hardship of country life. She had been Adèle's housekeeper for many decades, so long that she had stopped counting. She took pride in her work, her simplicity matched only by her decency, and not a minute passed that she did not bless the day Adèle took her in.

She led the way into the study through a small

corridor adorned with tapestries, whose softness contrasted with her stern expression. The burled-oak grandfather clock chimed three times as she ushered him into the study. Raising her luminous forehead, Adèle laid her long hand on the large leather-bound volume pressed in her lap, pausing her study of the botanical drawing of St. John's Wort.

Debasse muttered, he was just passing by. Without waiting for a response, he walked towards the velvet sofa facing the chimney and Adèle's old fashioned armchair— her favorite resting spot after her long morning walks. Her almond-shaped cornflower blue eyes closed slightly as a sign of acknowledgment. She was no dupe; he rarely ventured this way. This was no social visit. Nor was he here to delight in the moist caramel walnut tart that had established Bernadine's reputation as an unrivaled cook. Debasse rubbed his hands together in a slow deliberate motion and then got straight to the point.

Did she know that rumors of vagrants cutting down trees and illegally hunting had been circulating for weeks in neighboring villages? Fences had been knocked down or ripped open. A few days before, local farmers had visited Debasse complaining that their crops were being destroyed. Of course, many attributed the damage to the wild boar that had been haunting the region for decades. It had recently been sighted.

Others were alarmed at the recent claims that these miscreants had destroyed Didier's vineyard and set his barn on fire—a serious affair, as every year this cheerful and generous man shared his regionally acclaimed Malbec with the entire village. No one ignored the lamentations of the *Bouchère* who, on her way back from a morning errand delivering lamb chops across the river, had come face to face with a strange lunatic with a disturbing, enigmatic glow in his eyes. Obviously, she was hysterical over this frightening experience. But now, her distressing account had ballooned out of control, and was the center of gossip at Brévin's, the local café. Of course, Debasse had quickly reacted by reassuring the community and calling for a municipal council. Léonard, the mayor's right-hand man, had been summoned immediately to lend a strong hand to patrol the area.

Adèle sat still, her gaze distant, circumspect. She paused at the mention of Léonard, a skilled hunter. She was disturbed by the idea that strangers might be roaming and poaching in the nearby woods. Besides being illegal, poaching was regarded by locals as one of the gravest sins against man and Nature. To them, land was sacred for the owners to enjoy—an unspoken and unbreakable rule. Although authorities rarely penalized violations, locals believed that poachers would receive their just desserts by way of Nature's inherent moral system.

In fact, Adèle could still remember when, decades back, the village blacksmith had shamelessly sold glossy partridges and furry hares on market days, passing them as his own. A few days later, he had a terrible and inexplicable fall. His shop soon fell silent, and bankruptcy followed.

Noticing Adèle's distraction, Debasse tapped his index finger on the armrest. Lifting it in the air, he resumed with *élan*.

She *must* understand that the problem was further compounded by the pilgrims, who, on their way to St. James' pilgrimage via Rocamadour, walked along the cow paths that irrigated the countryside like a network of arteries. And frankly, he gesticulated, one could only fear that things would get worse if the pilgrims were left to their own devices. These cow paths had become the perfect avenue for outlaws, poachers and criminals, allowing them to travel undetected. As the mayor of Calignac, he took as his foremost priority the village's safety; the situation clearly called for immediate action. And there was only one solution to that disturbing problem, he trailed off, daring to wink at her from under his bushy eyebrows.

Debasse was now pacing up and down, convinced that his grandiloquence was persuasive. Then he sat back down again, adrenaline pulsing through his veins. He cocked his head to the side, expecting a reaction. But Adèle stared at him in silence, filled with an unassailable resolve which Debasse mistook for an invitation to expound further on the topic.

He continued: the main path, that is, the artery that led down to the village, must be closed permanently without further delay. In fact, she would not be surprised to find out that many landowners, like her, had already approved of his initiative. He had come today to ask for her official support, the support he needed to see this motion through at the counsel and ensure the security of their community.

He finally paused and stared at her. Adèle smoothed out the pleats of her gray flannel skirt, elongating her neck as she often did when sitting too long. She met his dark gaze and smiled.

CHAPTER THREE

Down in the verdant valley, leaning on his knotted cane, Finoud made his way through the forest along a secluded trail. He walked, the fresh air engulfing his entire body. He paused at times to acknowledge the details of the path he knew so well, savoring the serenity that had become his daily luxury. His joints often ached—Montrelazet, the village *Docteur,* had warned him it could be an onset of gout despite his ascetic diet.

Finoud stopped only to rub his hands with careful gentleness, gazing at the fields on one side and the woods on the other. He took in the fullness of the moment. A few leaves rustled with the summer breeze, rolling down the hill over the drying alfalfa, eventually funneling into the green and dense stretch of moss-covered oak trees below.

His swollen knuckles still served him well, he chuckled to himself. They wove chairs and carved wood clogs with the same eagerness he had known all his life. Putting his hand to his mouth, he called Béatrice, his devoted white and black Border Collie who helped lead his sheep herd over the hills and vales. This purposeful meandering with Béatrice was the salt of his existence. Spirited yet docile, his companion trotted along, sparing no effort to please her master. She barked back several times as if to confirm Finoud's request in *patois*, the local dialect of this region of southwest France. Villagers recognized her distinct throaty barks in the distance, punctuated by the languorous peals of the village bells, which sounded at dusk as the white limestone cliffs became inundated with the orange and purple glow of sunset.

Leaving the trail behind, he carefully stepped onto the little stone wall that separated the woods from the fields. A familiar sight to the locals, these little stone walls emerged from the lingering mist above the sun-drenched fields, a reminder of their mooring to the past, a past that enveloped their souls, like the velvety green moss that draped each stone so delicately. One could not help but marvel at these constructions springing from the ground. Over the centuries, it was the work of young shepherds who, while tending to their herds, had dug up, collected, and assembled small and large stones into these strong and rolling partitions that now delineated the countryside of the *Quercy* region.

Pivoting on a flat stone at the top, Finoud stepped down from the wall with the agility and lightness characteristic of an eternally youthful spirit. The weather looked good for the next few days, he thought, noticing how high the swallows flew. The tall grass swished by him as he walked up the field where the sheep grazed. As he looked up, he spotted Adèle's house which, from a distance, rose up imposing and tranquil, seemingly untouched by two centuries of wet winters and scorching summers. Time was a funny thing, for it seemed like yesterday when he first met Adèle.

He remembered the winter when the war was raging. Rationing was in effect. Bread, flour, butter, and sugar were in dire shortage, and despite a supply of ration tickets, the times were harsh. He could still picture Adèle standing before him, graceful despite her shabby gray coat. They had waited in line at the bakery for hours in the bitter cold. When Adèle's turn came, a sharp voice barked out that her tickets were no longer valid. Her shoulders sank, almost imperceptibly.

Wait! Had she not dropped these? Finoud had reached down to pick up ration tickets that had magically appeared on the ground at his feet. These must be yours, he insisted.

Containing her surprise, she bowed with gratitude at the stranger who had so generously given up his tickets without expecting anything in return.

Having recently lost her son and daughter-in-law, both killed in a bombing raid in Paris, she was now the sole guardian of Mathilde—a six-month old, wailing bundle of joy. The light rose-colored rationing coupons were worth gold in those days of scarcity. Now, she would be able to feed the baby properly. This was the first of many acts of kindness that led to a tight and deep friendship between the two: a bond stronger than the delightfully scented wisteria that now held the old garden archway together, springing back each year more resilient and fragrant than ever.

In the distance, the dormers resembled watchful stubborn eyes, with their white slotted shutters gazing out from the roofline to the Dordogne River. Finoud enjoyed the feeling of his feet sinking into the dirt as the soil gently yielded under the pressure of his deliberate steps. The recent news about Adèle or Bonne-Maman, as Mathilde affectionately called her, had been a shock. It had taken Finoud a few days to recover from the discovery of the ominous diagnosis that Montrelazet, the village *Docteur*, had pronounced. Yet Finoud did not question nature; rather, he embraced it, determined to support his friend with the same unwavering loyalty that had helped them weather many storms.

He knew that Adèle worried. Mathilde, now almost eleven, was becoming more temperamental, unpredictably swinging from reason to madness, as Bernadine would say, explaining it away as the fate of adolescence. But a lot more was at stake for Adèle, who deplored that Mathilde nonchalantly shrugged off her chores, slipping away like sand in her palm. When Adèle explained that the house and land needed tending, Mathilde stared into the distance with a stubborn pout. She did not seem to understand the necessity behind managing what her grandmother called "the gift" that this land bestowed on the family. She refused to do household chores, going on afternoon escapades whenever the mood struck, neglecting any tasks at hand. She always returned safe and sound, but her carelessness and frequent disappearances tormented her grandmother.

Adèle loved her grandchild with a wholehearted wisdom and devotion that stemmed from a long life of trials, of knowing what is of value in life. At night, she worried that she was losing her connection with Mathilde. Her common sense told her that Mathilde's behavior was surely part of growing up. But, in light of the recent downturn in her health, a newfound sense of urgency had taken hold.

It was with this knowledge that she had reached out to Finoud, the only person she would have trusted with her life and the child that she had vowed to raise. He was the only one capable of helping impart to Mathilde what she called *la sagesse de la terre*—the wisdom of the earth. Only Finoud could make Mathilde understand that loving nature and honoring life and loved ones left no room for ego. He would make her see that love is bound to service, and that it was her duty to protect the land that she roamed so freely and carelessly.

And so, each time dark thoughts and misgivings plagued Adèle, she clung to her deep-rooted conviction that, with Finoud's help, things would ultimately fall into place.

CHAPTER FOUR

oachers and criminals? Adèle repeated, returning to
the present moment as she sat across from
Debasse. But my dear friend, she continued, her
lips widening with a smile, a man of your position could
not possibly credit all these rumors. Your role as leader is
to shed light on the untoward nature of these events—to
separate fact from fiction. You must be the voice of *reason*
in Calignac. Indeed, the *Bouchère* was known for her wild
ramblings and even if most were entertained by her
operatic performances, no one took her words seriously.
How could he? As for the fire at Didier's barn, it had
started up on the roof and Didier was the first to admit
that lightning was most likely the cause.

Rash decisions often led to foolishness, Adèle mused
aloud almost as if to herself. There was no doubt that
besides undermining its obvious religious *raison d'être,*
closing the main path would be detrimental to the

community in more ways than one. The paths were a common way of traveling through the countryside for locals and neighboring villagers. The *Fête de la Truffe* was just three months away. How could he seriously entertain the idea of closing the path at such a critical time for the village? She was sure it would jeopardize access to Calignac and compromise the success of the year's biggest event.

Debasse heaved a big sigh and squirmed in his seat, suddenly restless or annoyed, Adèle could not quite tell. His eyebrows drooped ever so slightly. When he had mulled over the details of his plan, he had considered the downsides, but dismissed them quickly. He was a man of action, after all. In that moment, he was unnerved that Adèle's objections resurrected his earlier reservations.

Adèle noticed his expression but continued anyway. Had he consulted Trouvert? She pressed on, knowing full well that he had not. In fact, Trouvert would have a fit when he learned of Debasse's plans, she thought. On All Saints' Day, Trouvert led a religious procession down the cow path to the Dordogne River and ended the festivities in Calignac after circling the village.

The mayor sat up, battling an oppressive sensation in his chest. Despite his relative overall health, years of smoking often caught up with him. His mind was racing. Trouvert, yes, he had overlooked Trouvert… He could feel his heart pulsing through the carotid in his neck. An uneasy silence fell over the room. He ran his hand along the rim of the hat in his hand, back and forth, for what seemed like a long minute, and then he slowly got up, puffing with repressed anger.

Yes, there was a lot to consider, and the community still had to make some headway with the project, he said, irked by her objection. So far, the damage had been limited to a few fields, but frankly, there was no telling what would happen next, he muttered under his breath. More vagrants and pilgrims would come—and who could make the difference between the two when the long shadows roamed at night?

With the damage Calignac had witnessed in the last few days, the villagers' nagging feelings of insecurity were not likely to subside so easily. In fact, it was only going to get worse; it was a matter of time before drifters started looting the entire countryside. If Adèle did not join in her support, she could soon become a victim of vandalism, poaching, or both. She would regret not acting sooner to protect her land, he warned.

What could he do to convince her of the urgency of the situation? Her beautiful, wooded vale that stretched beyond the stone walls down below would be next. Was she ready to take that risk with the land that had been in her family for generations? He glimpsed at Adèle but could not penetrate the imperturbable smoothness of her grave expression.

Debasse rose to his feet. Of course, he would give her time to think about it—but not too much, he stressed, heading to the door. His heavy steps turned into a soft shuffle, and then the house fell back to its familiar peace, punctuated by the merry ticking of the large grandfather clock in the entrance.

Adèle leaned back and pondered the mayor's performance with amused disbelief.

What had this visit truly been about? Was Debasse really asking for her support to close the paths? Was this a new strategy to prepare for his campaign and possible re-election? Appealing to villagers' fears while promising safety and order had always been the mark of power-hungry leaders.

Or did he have something else up his sleeve? Could it be that he wanted the path for himself? She could not be sure, but something was brewing.

She had to see Finoud.

CHAPTER FIVE

A week had passed since Adèle had called Finoud to recount the mayor's visit and proposition. The two friends had agreed that Debasse's passionate defense of the path was suspicious. Although it made sense from a pragmatic perspective, they had learned that Debasse never did anything because it was the right thing to do. He was only motivated by his personal agenda and insatiable ambitions as he always was. Finoud had promised Adèle to keep an ear out. Debasse's plan to close the path would not be met with indifference, and in the tight and opinionated community of Calignac, people would talk.

Clouds rolled in from the west. This usually meant that a storm was fast approaching up the Dordogne Valley, Finoud thought, adjusting his black woolen *béret*. He had been right to keep his herd safe in shelter that morning. He was on his way to Adèle's to meet with

Mathilde to teach her about the soil and the land that she would one day own: what he called his *leçon de choses*.

After passing Bonne-Maman's orchard, its trees loaded with ripening pears and apples, Finoud gave a light knock on the kitchen door and found Bernadine sitting on a wooden bench inside the *cantou*—the old-fashioned stone fireplace that occupied an entire wall, its dark andirons heavily coated with soot. She was canning plums, and a large *marmite* hung down from the trammel over the hearth. Finoud looked around for Mathilde but saw only Bernadine.

The girl's mood had apparently taken yet another unexpected turn after lunch, as she had disappeared without a word. Bonne-Maman was beside herself, Bernadine explained with exasperation, for it pained her to see Adèle struggle. Finoud gave Bernadine a knowing look. A black boar had been sighted near Calignac a few weeks before. This unusual beast was very dangerous, known for its lethal attacks; rumor had it that this creature harbored a sixth sense, a formidable instinct that allowed it to thwart men's tricks and avoid traps. Understandably, Adèle was worried sick about Mathilde's daily outings, especially her escapades at dusk, a time when wild boars like to search for food, Finoud thought. No need to worry, Mathilde was probably off with the neighbor's boy down near the wooded vale, he offered with a smile, trying to reassure Bernadine.

And he was right. Mathilde had followed Bruno, the neighbor's son down the orchard. After the night's rain, the cow path down by the wooded vale had flooded, and it glittered in the distance. Puddles had merged into a small stream below the dense canopy of oak trees.

Better than staying home, he chuckled with a twinkle in his eyes. Mathilde could not agree more, as she hopped from one stone to the next.

Flushed with excitement, she leaned forward to watch the toads swelling with their shiny white bellies, the dragonflies shimmering with blue light, and the golden beetles scurrying for higher ground. Her legs tingled with pleasure. Bruno was standing in front of her, grinning from under his dark locks of hair, free like the summer wind. His mother, Madame Sardelois, could not manage to keep him at home, either. The more she tightened her grip on him, the more he eluded her with his incorrigible *joie de vivre*. Mathilde related to the feeling of being constricted, especially lately, as things had not been quite the same in the household since the beginning of summer. With Finoud's weekly visits to *work on her education*, as Bonne-Maman put it, Mathilde was puzzled by the urgency she sensed in Finoud's instruction: the same seriousness that she read on her grandmother's enigmatic brow.

As Bruno headed towards the vale, Mathilde could not tune out Bonne-Maman's words. They echoed in her mind as she lagged behind her companion. *Rules were rules.* But Bruno's contagious laughter was irresistible, pulling her closer to the vale, the place dearest to her heart. It was not long before they reached the wall, climbed over it, and entered the piece of land known as a safe haven for wildlife. Because it was Adèle's prized possession, she had enlisted the assistance of Gérard, a rugged and burly man, to keep poachers at bay. Besides tending to the orchard, pruning trees, weeding, and fixing walls and fences, he was instructed to watch the vale and report any suspicious activity. The children often encountered him checking for traps. But today, he was nowhere to be seen.

As they walked deeper into the thickness of the wood, they detected a strange moaning sound in the distance. It was a painful whine, a pleading cry coming from amid the green undercover. Bruno grabbed Mathilde's hand, but she held back for a second, a shiver running down her spine. Could it be the wild boar? When they reached the middle of the vale, the sun was casting shadows mottled with pools of light. They stood still for a moment, wide-eyed, scanning the grounds. And then they spotted it.

There, beyond the branches and brambles, a faint beam of light revealed a splash of red.

CHAPTER SIX

Mathilde stared at the young female fox they had been trailing for months. Just a few feet away, the fox winced with pain as she tried to free her bleeding foot from the jaws of a well-crafted trap. The more she pulled on her tangled bloody limb, the more the snare tightened. Gérard had done his rounds. How did he miss that? Mathilde wondered with surprise.

The animal, with an unusual maroon cruciform mark on its head, met their gaze head on. It stood there, motionless, its black nose to the wind trying to gauge the intent of these two unexpected visitors. What should they do? If they took another step, the fox could be severely injured. But suddenly the animal turned its head to the right, ears pricked up, its entire body contracting with renewed alarm. The children peered in the distance, tracking the rustle of leaves. Someone was coming.

From the thicket emerged a dark and imposing slab of a silhouette. It was Léonard. If Bonne-Maman only knew?! Mathilde shuddered recalling Bernadine's frequent warnings of Léonard. He did Debasse's dirty jobs, and many thought him to be a ruthless man devoid of morals. He hunted like a brute, with no care or appreciation for the game he brought back.

Léonard approached, and his dark eyes zoomed in on them. Swift and menacing, he took a step toward the trapped fox and shifted his entire weight into a kneeling position. Squeezing each other's hands, the children shrank back in fear.

The hunter now had his powerful hands on the animal's neck, holding its graceful body firmly against the ground. In a matter of seconds, his hand reached for the hunting blade hanging by his belt. The metal glinted in the sparse sunbeams coming through the trees. Mathilde's vision seemed to blur for a brief second as if dazed by the magnetic physical presence of the man. Swallows screeched high in the blue sky. And then in a swift motion, Léonard's strong shovel-like hands unexpectedly ripped apart the snare. His face folded into a bearish smile. Bah! This was the second time he rescued it this week, he nodded, shrugging his shoulders.

They watched the fox falter into the bushes, its steps unsteady and strained by its wound. Léonard stood up, and Mathilde gripped Bruno's hand. Then, in a slow guttural voice, the hunter proceeded to recount how he had come to check on the mayor's hen house, but had changed course when he heard the growling. These traps were despicable—whoever set them up was lucky not to have run into the likes of himself. Appearances were truly misleading, Léonard admitted, interpreting the children's silent hesitation. He knew that locals talked about his supposedly shady past since he arrived in Calignac a few years ago, but these rumors were unfounded. Nobody had ever really taken the time to understand his situation. No one would touch that fox if he had anything to do with it, he grunted.

Mathilde's fear suddenly melted away and her dewy eyes softened into a timid smile. She remembered that it was important to give others the benefit of the doubt, just as we hope others would do for us. Dismissing Bruno's tug to leave, Mathilde stepped forward, eager to share her love for the fox. Like Léonard, she had been watching the animal, tracking its daily whereabouts.

In the morning, Clémentine—as she had named the fox—skipped over the stony wall into the vale, her feet hardly touching the mossy stones, her silky fur glowing in the warm sun like a lit torch. In the afternoons, she lay languorously in the soft, high grass, surveying the grounds for prey.

Later in the day, often at dusk, she roamed the vale in search of fresh eggs that she stole from bird nests. Crouched amid the caramel foliage, she would wait, listening intently, her red hair bristling in the breeze. Then she would suddenly dart through the bushes and pounce on careless rodents. What amazed Mathilde most was that Clémentine seemed to be able to pinpoint the precise location of her prey, even when it was below ground.

Léonard grimaced into a half smile as he listened attentively. He seemed willing to continue the conversation when they heard leaves rustling in the distance. His entire frame became rigid, and his dark eyes narrowed into ominous slits. Maybe a dog in the distance, he muttered, on the alert.

One last thing, the hunter continued. No one could ever know that they had spoken and most of all, that he had freed the fox, he said, leaning forward to swear them to silence. Especially the trap. Debasse had hired him to protect his hens and *not* the fox. If the mayor ever found out that Léonard had repeatedly freed the fox, Debasse would haul him over the coals. *No one,* he finished in a mutter that was soon lost in the depth of the vale.

CHAPTER SEVEN

Saturday morning, leaning forward with his arms behind his back, Debasse walked around the bustling market. Today was a special day. He wore the starched cream-colored shirt he saved for special occasions, and the pin-striped suit that concealed his bulging belly. At eleven o'clock sharp, he would ring the ancestral bell that stood in front of St. Calin's fountain to announce the big celebration that galvanized the whole community every December. Today, the official countdown would begin and in just ninety days, Calignac would host the region's most anticipated event of the year: the *Fête de la Truffe*.

Since Debasse's election as town mayor, the fair had changed significantly. Once a simple celebration centered on the spirit of St. Calin, and a poetic celebration of nature's most prized possession, the dark truffles of the region, it now included more gaudy entertainment at the expense of fewer small food producers and local crafts-men. This new direction had generated a lot of criticism from the elders and Madame Sardelois, Bruno's mother, who argued that the garish extra nonsense detracted from the deep meaning of the *Fête de la Truffe*.

But Debasse shrugged it off. He felt that hosting flashy attractions would keep visitors entertained and merchants happy. His term was up, and he would soon be seeking a re-appointment. He felt confident that boosting the *Fête*'s attendance and generating soaring profits would prove his capacity as a leader of the community. What better measure of success?

Instead of checking his watch one more time, Debasse decided to distract himself and pass by the *Bouchère*. She was no doubt a force to be reckoned with, but luckily, she had been on his side since he had taken office. In fact, since his election four years ago, she had been managing all logistics for the *Fête de la Truffe* and this year, once again, she would organize the event. She loved being in the limelight, and had dethroned her predeces-sor, the *Boulangère*. More importantly, it gave her the chance to get closer to Debasse whom she believed was one of the most brilliant minds. Of course, there were these persistent rumors about decadent and wasteful dinners held for a happy few at his home, but she dismissed them as unfounded accusations.

Kissing him on both cheeks, she handed him a small basket of mushrooms and casually slipped into his shirt pocket a brown envelope that Léonard had left on her doorstep at dawn. Debasse grinned greedily at the trove of pungent and golden mushrooms—most likely *cèpes* and *chanterelles*. The best mushrooms she had found this season, she said with feigned modesty. He politely excused himself. His rounds were not over, and he wanted to properly assess the competition, he joked with some seriousness. The *Bouchère* nodded, approving of Debasse's professionalism—although rumor had it that there might not be any contender at all for the mayor's position. Debasse strolled to the other side of the square, to greet local merchants near Brévin's café, opposite the church. With his usual garrulous ease, he greeted everyone with warm handshakes and spared no flattery. He stood there for a moment, observing the bustling activity of the marketplace.

Seeing Adèle stroll down the aisles on her errands triggered unresolved qualms surrounding their recent conversation. He could not get over her refusal. He wondered how to secure his motion, before the municipal council, to close the path without her vote.

A few days prior, he had met with Trouvert, hoping to garner his support. It was unclear what this man of God would recommend to the council on the day of the vote. The priest had walled himself into a somber silence and their exchange had left Debasse equally frustrated. As mayor, had he not advocated for the church roof to be replaced at the cost of the taxpayers? How could anyone really think that *he* was an enemy of the church? *Sacre bleu!* He was married to the pious Constance!

Indeed, his wife of ten years was known throughout the whole region for her deep religious fervor. Shameless, he was quick to claim the positive effects of her faith on his reputation as the result of his work ethic and social adroitness. Still, when he lay awake at night listening to her soft breathing, her devotion gnawed at him.

Debasse frowned and tried to distract himself from these unpleasant thoughts, scanning the colorful and lively crowd that filled the town square. There was one redeeming piece of news. That morning, he had received confirmation from Paris that Courteline, his gourmet friend, would attend the *Fête de la Truffe, his Fête de la Truffe.*

They had first met at Austerlitz Station in Paris a few years back. It had been a wonderful chance encounter, when Debasse had mistakenly grabbed Courteline's suitcase. Debasse had taken the dandy's amused smile of condescension at his uncouthness as a sign of favor, as if someone had finally recognized his cosmopolitan *savoir-vivre.* The memory of this pivotal moment in his destiny solidified his belief that he was on the right path. Courteline would help Debasse achieve his wildest dreams.

This year, he would make the Parisian an offer he could not resist.

CHAPTER EIGHT

Standing in front of the *Bouchère*'s stall, Adèle browsed the display of meats, checking to make sure her grandchild was still following her. Mathilde was sullenly trailing in her wake, resentful that her escapade in the wood had gotten her in such trouble. This time, her disobedience and failure to meet Finoud had sent her grandmother over the edge. Mathilde was grounded for the next three weeks. She could not even see Bruno. But what she missed most, besides running freely in the fields, was the little fox, Clémentine. She prayed that no harm had come to the animal after it had been released from the trap.

Adèle looked around. Debasse's forthcoming announcement about the *Fête de la Truffe* was all the buzz, the *Bouchère* commented as she selected a few blood puddings.

Yes, and the issue of the Pilgrims' Path was on everyone's lips, Adèle added.

Had she heard the rumors? the *Bouchère* went on. Two of the mayor's hens had disappeared and just yesterday, Didier, the local winemaker, had discovered that the ripest grapes in his vineyard had mysteriously vanished. Vagrants again, no doubt, the *Bouchère* tsked indignantly. This was outright theft! And what most did not realize was that the Bouchère's property was next to Didier's, along the Pilgrims' Path. There was no telling what would happen next; this trespassing had to stop. And if Adèle wanted to know, there was no question that she was going to support Debasse's proposal to close all cow paths, she proclaimed with self-importance. Adèle gazed back with polite indifference.

At the center of the square, Debasse checked his watch again. Patience was not one of his strong suits. As the church bells pealed the last stroke of eleven, he climbed atop the makeshift dais. A whisper rippled across the square and all eyes focused on him. Erect, Debasse surveyed the crowd, holding a brass hammer to strike the old brass bell. He loved the rush of power he felt as he prepared to galvanize the community around the preparations for the *Fête de la Truffe*.

Calignac would again rise to heights of fame, drawing crowds of eager visitors, he began. He paused, imagining how the surrounding villages would recognize his pioneering role in creating an epic contribution for future generations. He continued aloud: this year, the fair would be a pure sensation, thanks to his own dogged determination, and a few clever arrangements. Debasse continued in this vein, energized by the sound of his own voice.

In a dramatic gesture, he concluded his speech, leaning forward in an attempt to catch everyone's eye, and then rang the bell. The crowd broke into applause, and a vain smile crept across the deep furrows of his jaws.

Adèle had been listening to Debasse's speech with half an ear. Always the same self-glorifying monologue, she thought. Change was good, indeed. Especially when it meant the *Fête de la Truffe* would receive increased recognition and acclaim as the most important event for food lovers and connoisseurs alike. But, since his election, Debasse had gradually turned it into a bazaar awash with entertainers and cheap merchandise. As their stalls came back up for lease, market merchants now faced a fierce bidding battle.

As a result, local producers and small craftsmen were inexorably being priced out, replaced by low-quality stalls, relegated to become stragglers that leeched on the edges of the village fairgrounds. Adèle was pained to see St. Calin's legacy debased and its centuries-old spirit flouted in such a flippant manner. She knew she was not the only one to feel this way. Others were concerned but few were willing to speak up. Madame Sardelois had been shocked by Debasse's ballooning ambition and in response, she hinted that she might run for mayor.

A few cumulus clouds parted, and sunlight landed at the nape of Adèle's neck, diffusing along her shoulder bones. The light flashed past her, landing on the *Bouchère's* brass scales, then blossoming into a steady golden beam. She watched, entranced as the cheery rays capered around onto other parts of the stall, reflecting off metal cans and preserves. Adèle loved this feeling of elation such moments gave her, when all came to a standstill, with the marketplace hustle and hubbub seemingly fading away and eventually disappearing. She could feel her breathing slowing down as she tried to capture that moment of calmness with her thoughts gently relenting and quietening down.

Her gaze moved further along the stall and then stopped on a soft feathery mound: rust and ochre shimmering with a radiant glow, golden brown and deep black streaks weaving through patches of sky blue. Its tail, long and regal, lay fanned in golden-brown splendor, its intricate black barring a testament to its short-lived splendor. Her breath caught—its head, moiré with deep blue and crowned with a greenish-gray patch, was cocked to the side, the crimson wattles dull against its limp form. Its golden eyes stared blankly past the milling crowd, and its ivory beak hung slightly open, as if frozen mid-protest. She noticed its bloody leg, tucked modestly under its body. Quite unusual on a fowl, she mused, a heavy weight in her chest. She recognized the Bouchère's bird. She could see how it had desperately tried to yank itself free. Could it be the one that she had seen the day before in the vale? She had an odd feeling in her gut, one that she could not suppress.

CHAPTER NINE

Steeped in the dimmed tranquility of the late afternoon, Bonne-Maman sat at the long farm table over a heavy porcelain bowl of chamomile tea. She gazed at the large bouquet of cornflowers that Madame Sardelois had brought her that morning. Her stomach was unsettled; her nausea and coughing were not improving.

While she stirred the silver spoon amid the floating heads of chamomile flowers, the image of the small pheasant in the *Bouchère*'s stall swirled through her mind. Suddenly, in a moment of incredible sharpness, she let out a gasp, her heart pulsing. She saw the invisible line connecting all the fleeting elements that her unconscious mind had been trying to piece together.

This *was* the pheasant she had seen just a couple of days ago! Indeed, that day, she had decided to inspect the condition of the old stone wall along the Pilgrims' Path.

Her eyes had darted into the vale as if drawn by the silent depth of the verdant domain whose secrets she had kept in her heart since she was a little girl.

Right away, she had spotted that small pheasant on the mossy underwood; it lay there, a soft and limp bundle, its legs caught in a steel trap among the oak trees that distinguished the clearing. The deep blue sheen of its feathers was unmistakable. The pheasant's head was tilted to the side, as if about to take flight at any second. But blood was oozing from its beak, revealing the reality of the situation: evidence of cruel and unlawful traps. Adèle's entire body shivered as an acrid burn filled her throat.

She added a lump of sugar to cut the bitterness and carefully walked back to the library, holding her warm cup in the darkness. It was as if every step on the worn parquet floor brought her back to the memory of that frightful sight. It still haunted her body, deep in her gut. In fact, she remembered vividly how the mayor had come in that very same day to make his passionate proposal for the closing of the Pilgrims' Path. What nerve! she exclaimed to herself, as she entered the softness of the room, drawn by the glowing afternoon sun. *Dieu merci*, she had spoken to Finoud; his advice was always invaluable. Suspicious things were happening in that vale, and she suspected this was not the end of it—in fact, quite the opposite.

CHAPTER TEN

Adèle took a seat in her favorite leather armchair. That September morning, Bernadine had moved it to face the two large French windows which opened onto an expansive stone terrace. Leaning back, she enjoyed the gentle heat for it reminded her of the hot summer days when her skin drank the balmy and earthy breeze rising from the Dordogne River. She knew it so well, this distinctive humidity, characteristically paired with the intense summer heat radiating from the scorched white limestone plateau. Her mind drifted and she closed her eyes.

Everything was as he had predicted. She remembered with vividness her visit to the *Docteur*'s a few months before. She could still see him, perched on his puffy leather armchair, his short legs hanging behind his grandfather's large desk.

I am sure you know the meaning of this, he said. The words were catching in his throat. Of course, she had known. She had suspected it all along—the pain in her chest and the blood she had coughed up on several occasions. Montrelazet had mindlessly rubbed his spectacles on his suit, trying to conceal his emotions as he looked into her blue eyes. Years of medical experience hardly prepared him for the deep sadness that overwhelmed him.

How much time? Adèle had asked, gazing back at him with trusting kindness. There was no way of knowing for sure, he had answered her, softly reaching for her hand across the desk. She nodded, sensing how tough this moment was for him. Throwing her head back, she laughed a little at the irony of it all: she was past her youth, far beyond the age of playing a tragic heroine.

She stood up, thanked him and left. Her mind was racing, putting together the last few pieces of the puzzle that life had handed her. She had walked home unhurriedly. Letting go was a daily struggle, but she must accept the inevitable twist that her life had taken. Some days were easier than others.

The rays of the afternoon sun advanced on the honeyed parquet, like a gentle wave. She sat quietly, contemplating the movement as the leading edge of the sunlight progressed silently, first from her feet, until eventually her whole body was bathed in its exquisite warmth, glowing with insistence on her skin, radiating through her eyelids. The dazzling veil of energy engulfed her for a moment that lasted an eternity, until the floor yielded a soft moan to the pressure of footsteps.

Emerging from her vision, Adèle noticed Mathilde standing at the doorway of the terrace, her mid-length honey-colored hair gleaming in the sunlight. As if gliding across the polished surface, the green-eyed girl approached and hopped onto the wide armrest.

A mesmerizing smell of oak tree bark and honey-suckle surfaced from the wooded vale that lay below, beyond the orchard. The wonder of this land had to endure beyond her, Adèle mused. This earth that was outside yet forever inside her blood, bound to her soul. What would it take for Mathilde to feel and appreciate the wondrous world that surrounded them? Would her soul ever leap for joy at the sight of the wooded vale? She smiled, reaching out to ruffle through her granddaughter's wavy hair, but Mathilde had slipped off the armchair—just as Adèle's time was slipping away.

The clock chimed and Adèle suddenly realized she had been lost in her thoughts. Matilde was now long gone. She stood up and walked to the French doors. She stared at the beautiful wicker tree in the distance. Its stout figure stood among the fruit trees with its branches shooting up straight, like arrows aimed at the pearly white sky. It would yield long, strong branches for basket weaving. Next to it, Bernadine was collecting horsetails from the moist, sandy soil—she needed them to clean

Adèle's copper pots. Farther down, Mathilde was picking apples and pears. Since running away with Bruno, the little girl remained grounded until further notice. Keeping Mathilde focused on chores would keep her out of trouble.

Even from a hundred yards away, Adèle could detect Mathilde's resentment: she carelessly dropped fruit into the basket with that stubborn frown she wore when things did not go her way. At times, she took a long pause, and her body turned towards the vale. Maybe her mind was consumed by thoughts of the fox, Adèle thought to herself with a pang.

Adèle's eyes drifted for a while over the green expanse of trees, below the orchard. She was gripped by the sense that irreversible things were taking place deep within her beloved vale. Though she always remained skeptical of Debasse's motivations—as they did not see eye-to-eye on many issues—she was now starting to wonder whether his proposal to close the path was actually not a bad idea. Clearly, the pheasant was evidence of poachers, and on her land. Someone was flouting the rules, and limiting access might be an effective way to protect the vale. Could it be just what she needed to solve her problem? The idea that her interests aligned with those of Debasse made her uneasy.

A cool draft coming up from the Dordogne River made her retreat. She pulled a large woolen shawl over her shoulders and walked to the other side of the room. At the front of the house, lime-green heaps of walnuts mottled the red earth, a reminder that harvest time was near. She loved their fresh milky taste and Bernadine's special walnut *croquants*. In a month or so, Calignac would celebrate the *Fête de la Truffe,* and she would host a *soirée* for the entire village the evening after.

This year's might be the last.

CHAPTER ELEVEN

October came with its characteristic morning chill in the air. Mathilde was trying her best to stay on the straight and narrow. That day, she was sinking her teeth into a succulent pear when Bonne-Maman stepped into the kitchen. Adèle was in an indefinable state of mind, the kind that Mathilde could not read. Better avert her eyes and carry on, she thought, staring stubbornly at the delicately grainy flesh of the fruit.

Adèle led her grandchild into the study where they sat down on the sofa. Her grandmother's eyes seemed animated with a burning fire, as if they had seized upon some memory that they could not relinquish. Better not to speak, Mathilde thought. She could not tell whether her right foot was itching or falling asleep. She rolled her ankle to alleviate the discomfort, but soon the even cadence of Bonne-Maman's soft voice filled the empty space, rising and falling like the wind. The little girl's tensed muscles relaxed as she sat back, entranced by the rhythm and modulation of this voice that drew her in.

Bonne-Maman began: as strange as it might seem to Mathilde, change was the essence of life; it could not be avoided. Yes, there was no doubt that time often brought degradation, but it also guaranteed renewal. Leaves fell and rotted on the ground, but they also transformed into fertile compost. This was the necessary and ineluctable cycle of rebirth at the heart of Nature connecting us to our destiny. The earth that stretched before them would soon freeze and again be reborn just like wheat seeds would freeze to better germinate in the spring. Nothing could resist this unyielding change so it made sense to embrace it.

Behind these strange and sometimes abrupt changes lay a higher reason. If Trouvert called it God, she preferred to see it as a principle that guided the course of nature and life. One day, Mathilde would realize that if everything else around her crumbled in her hands, the land would endure. This land, the same deep red soil she played with as a child, was the connection between the past and the future, the one tangible thing that could give meaning to absurdity in times of hardship, she said, smiling down at Mathilde.

The wooded vale was a perfect example of this. It had been passed down in their family from generation to generation since the Renaissance. She, like the many generations before her, had been entrusted to safeguard this sanctuary and protect it against all harm, just as Mathilde would do one day. The love for this land burned deep inside of her. It had shaped her life, as it would shape Mathilde's.

But there was more, Adèle said, her voice hesitating, for a second. Her mind was racing; she was trying to find the right words. Leaning forward, she reached for the little girl's hand. She had sad news to share with Mathilde, she paused, clearing her throat. She already knew how painful it was going to be.

Mathilde's friend, the fox Clémentine, had been caught and killed, she explained, carefully choosing her words. Mathilde's lips quivered, her jaw muscles locked, and her little chest contracted. It seemed that she was going to choke; big tears started rolling down her rosy cheeks until she let out a fully-fledged sob of despair. Her entire body shook with grief; her restrained weeping suddenly became sobs of wild abandonment. How did she know? Was she sure? Mathilde managed to ask, almost inaudibly.

Yes, it was Clémentine, Adèle nodded reluctantly. Sensing Mathilde's disbelief, she carried on. Unfortunately, everything matched: there was no mistaking the fox's fur and the unique cruciform mark she bore on her head and neck. It was a female too, Adèle nodded reluctantly.

Mathilde's chest stiffened, stifled by the pain. The flames in the fireplace danced wildly as she tried to catch her breath. When? And who had committed such cruelty? she uttered.

Last night… Léonard, Adèle answered softly. The whole village had witnessed the hunter parading his trophy, his eyes shining with jubilation. Holding his bloody catch high for all to see, he had walked straight to Debasse's house to claim his bounty.

Léonard? Léonard!! The little girl repeated, struck into an agonizing stupor. She let out a sharp cry of disbelief as she collapsed further into her grandmother's lap.

Adèle straightened up as a realization flashed across her mind. Léonard's theatrics were cruel, and unnecessary…unless, of course, it was a direct attack on her.

CHAPTER TWELVE

Hours stretched into days; days flowed into weeks. The morning fog crept up to encircle the hilltop with its long and windy tail. Each day, it arrived a little earlier. The lapping sea of mist swayed eerily, penetrating even the smallest crevice between the gnarly knots of the ancient trees. It moved upward towards the edge of the wall, slowly progressing to eventually surround each of the apple trees in the orchard. With each sunrise and sunset, it grew nearer, closer, thicker.

Since breaking the news to Mathilde, a week ago, Adèle had caught a nasty cold, bronchitis with a high temperature and a deep raspy cough that would not let up. Montrelazet had left Bernadine a small opaque vial with strict instructions. Yes, a few drops at bedtime; Bernadine would follow the directions scrupulously. The benefits would not be instantaneous, but it would slowly ease Adèle's pain and get her back on her feet. The inflammation needed to subside—rest and rest again, he urged. But she *would* get better.

The news of the fox's death had shattered Mathilde. Her nights had become restless, her dreams haunted by dark menacing figures leaping at her from the tapestry that hugged the stone walls of her bedroom. When she emerged from her sleep, the morning light creeping under the heavy wooden shutters, she was suffocated by the knowledge of Léonard's treason.

In her dreams, she remembered his trained walk, silent and imperceptible, through the woods. Her eyes would fill with tears again. It was just so unfair and cruel. Although her little mind was plagued by the whys, she instinctively realized that it did not matter why, it just *was* and now she needed to face her feelings of guilt: she was directly responsible for Clémentine's demise. She had played into the hunter's hands with such naiveté, she thought, leaning on the cast-iron radiator behind the small windowpanes. How would she ever trust anyone else again? she wondered, recalling her grandmother's flair for extracting authenticity from confusion.

With Adèle bed-ridden, the house had become alarmingly quiet. Bernadine glided around on her felt slippers to buff the gleaming oak floors that she had just finished waxing, leaving behind a distinct scent of turpentine and honey. After school, Mathilde wandered over the dry hills and white cliffs until supper. Bernadine, who already had the whole house to look after, was incensed, realizing that the little girl was resuming her bad habits, flouting danger with the wild boar still out there.

Adèle spent most of her days in bed, her painful fits of coughing leaving her exhausted. Bernadine would bring her a cup of steaming *pot au feu* made from carrots, celery, potatoes, and a veal shank. Tucked beneath the white linen sheets, Adèle would sit up and ask: where was Mathilde? Bernadine invariably responded by raising a long silvery spoon to Adèle's lips. This broth worked miracles and time would do the rest, Bernadine reassured her, trying to elude her questions.

Time would have blurred completely, if not for Madame Sardelois' visits. She came every day to inquire about Adèle's health, but also to cheer Bernadine up. She never came empty-handed, always bringing a fruit compote or fresh *ratatouille* still steaming from her stove. Bernadine would voice her irritation at Adèle's helper, Gérard, who was neglecting his duties. Madame Sardelois would nod with sympathetic smiles.

Every day, he disappeared to the café for long hours, drowning in self-pity. Walnut *eau de vie* was his favorite. The rest of the time, he did nothing, not even watching the Pilgrims' Path or keeping an eye out for poachers in the vale, as Adèle had instructed him. But mostly, the two women talked about the children, Mathilde and Bruno. Running wild with disobedience, the two women grumbled with exasperation.

Bernadine finally managed to have a proper word

with the little girl. It was on a rainy afternoon and Bernadine was sitting at the table, peeling carrots and turnips when Mathilde walked in. So, she had come straight home from school today for a change? Could she not bear the rain!? Benardine started with derision. How could she disappear like that, leaving everyone worried sick, wondering if or when she would come back?

Mathilde quickly hung up her coat and sat down on the long wooden bench across from Bernadine without flinching. The little girl picked up an extra knife and began peeling a turnip in silence. A feeling of resentment mounted in her at having been found out.

The world did not revolve around her! Bernadine continued. If she thought for one minute that the bedridden Bonne-Maman was oblivious, she was dead wrong! Bernadine could not understand, Mathilde finally mumbled defensively. Ah *oui*, Bernadine said with her deep, strong voice. It was because of the incident with the fox, wasn't it? How could Mathilde imagine that no one had ever walked in her shoes? Everyone had lost something dear to them, everyone had at some point in their lives felt betrayed…

Bernadine went over to the heavy porcelain sink. The water ran for a while.

Mathilde kept her eyes locked on the pink edges of her turnip, angry at the world.

CHAPTER THIRTEEN

During the next few weeks, the days trickled away reluctantly as if the house and every-thing it contained were unwilling to register the passing of time. Bernadine was painfully aware that Bonne-Maman's health was not improving. Outside though, Nature followed its course. Bernadine had kept track of the walnut field in front of the house, noticing that with each day passing, walnuts were beginning to cover the red-earthed furrows of the field. With spring coming later than usual, the walnut harvest was delayed, affording Bernadine more time to gather neighbors around her in support of Adèle. This year more than ever, she felt relief that she could rely on this warm-hearted community to harvest the aged walnut trees across the road.

On a sunny morning, they all agreed to harvest Adèle's field until the ground was spotless and not a single hull was in sight. Leaning on his gnarled shepherd's stick, Finoud enjoyed orchestrating the whole affair, giving advice and directions, distributing gloves and baskets to Mathilde, Bruno and his mother, and all the neighbors who gathered around him.

Trouvert made the rounds, greeting everyone. His long cassock draping his gaunt figure, he blessed the fields and the spirit of generosity that inspired neighbors to work together. He smiled, listening to Finoud encouraging everyone to wear protection for their hands, knowing well how permanent the stain from the walnut husks could be. After a first pass, tarps were laid under each tree and the branches shaken vigorously to dislodge the last nuts. The dark fabrics quickly became speckled with green polka-dots. Once harvested, the walnuts would be placed out to dry for a few extra weeks, until the hulls burst naturally.

Not only did Finoud supervise the harvest, but he also managed to enchant the children with his tales about the earth. Walnuts were not just a good source of income; they taught villagers that nothing went to waste. Like Russian nesting dolls, the husks revealed their extraordinary properties, with each husk more complex and purposeful than the previous one. The inside kernel was eaten, the hull used as a stain, and the shell made excellent kindling. Loaded with tannins, juglandine, citric and malic acids, the husk was also used to create a concoction for upset stomachs. Although these natural remedies were often dismissed by modern medicine, the villagers of St. Calin could testify to their virtues.

But why were oak and walnut trees both surrounded by barren circles? the children asked, bright-eyed. True, Finoud agreed, both trees bore a strange resemblance to each other in that their roots rendered the soil around them infertile, but of course only oak trees birthed the most coveted truffles.

Mathilde grinned with delight, pressing Finoud for more details. Like many children in the village, she craved information about the mysterious truffles, these much-coveted mushrooms that the elders whispered about, a twinkle in their eyes. Finoud was happy to oblige. What was certain was that these underground fungi were regarded as akin to a gold mine and guarded like family treasure. The secret of their location was passed on from generation to generation, with much circumspection. Indiscreet questions about their origin were carefully eluded and their secrets prudently guarded.

The children nodded solemnly as they remembered hearing about a box of truffles that had been stolen from the *Bouchère* the previous week. The villagers' empathetic silence had made the children realize the gravity of such a theft. One day, they hoped they might be fortunate enough to unearth one of those precious specimens.

The last day of work was the most challenging because the slope at the end of the field was the steepest. One thing had changed, though, and raised everyone's morale: news of Adèle's slowly returning health was spreading. Neighbors had even spotted Adèle's silhouette at her bedroom window. They were delighted to hear that a warm meal awaited them at Adèle's house. Once all tarps were neatly folded and stored away, they walked over, the brisk chill of dusk brushing over their shoulders as the sun lowered beyond the white cliffs in the distance.

While the children lagged behind, enthused by a shiny beetle that had landed on Bruno's shoulder, there was a flash in the distance. A streak of light, a dissonant vision—Léonard flew by, astride a brand-new motorcycle. Mathilde quivered only to hear Finoud whispering in her ear: ill-gotten, ill-spent.

Was this an omen?

CHAPTER FOURTEEN

From the doorstep, Bernadine greeted her neighbors with open arms, a canvas apron tied around her wide waist. Looking into their weary faces, she smiled, knowing that the feast she had spent all day preparing would restore their strength and repay them for the kindness of helping her when she needed it most. She was especially comforted to see Adèle walking about the house that day. The harvest had been completed in time, which was a real load off Bernadine's shoulders.

Mathilde's diligent work during the harvest made Bernadine proud. The little girl had worked as intently as any of the adults: first to start and last to finish. She was pleasantly surprised, given Mathilde's careless meandering and defiant silence in the last months. No doubt, she was starting to come around. It could well be that the fox's sad fate had triggered something in the little girl's mind. Although the old woman would never have wished for it, she also knew that misfortunes in life can be great teachers. Bernadine could not wait to share this encouraging news with Adèle: Mathilde was growing up.

In the large kitchen, a feast waited by the hearth. The long oak table had been laid with thick porcelain country plates. Numerous chairs circled the large stone chimney mantle where huge logs crackled in a vibrant fire. A roasted leg of lamb sprinkled with rosemary and garlic was cooking in the oven and white *coco* beans simmered on the stove in a large cast-iron pot. Baskets of fresh bread and peppered *saucissons* were passed around as an appetizer.

Bernadine had even grilled some fresh black pudding on a bed of wood ashes. This blood pudding had been made from a large pig slaughtered for the *Fête de la Truffe*, its fresh fat a key ingredient in many of the dishes she would soon prepare. The large kitchen was buzzing with warm and animated conversations, all laughing as they ate and drank. They congratulated each other heartily over a job well done. Bernadine went around for refills. Finoud tended to the fire while Madame Sardelois cut more *saucisson* to replenish the serving platters. They had finished eating the lamb when soft steps were heard. Adèle appeared, bundled in a large blanket. Her face was wan and her features drawn, but her eyes had regained some of their mischievous liveliness. Bernadine immediately rushed over to help her to the bench beside the hearth—the one she favored because it kept her out of drafts.

As the party hummed away, Adèle tapped her glass gently with a fork to attract everyone's attention. Her recent fatigue had worried many, but they were reassured to see her up and about.

She thanked them all for their hard work and for coming to share this special moment that marked another prosperous year of harvesting. Here lay the real strength of Calignac, its people coming together to— She was cut short by the sound of the kitchen door being flung open.

All heads turned in surprise. It was Gérard, his hair in disarray and eyes wide like saucers, looking dazed and deranged. What had finally awakened him from his drunken stupor at Brévin's? Bernadine wondered, frustrated by his inconsistencies. His lack of dependability in previous weeks had been an unnecessary burden on the household during Adèle's "indisposition," as she called it.

He had run all the way back from the town hall with breaking news, he panted. The mayor had managed to get the municipal council to ratify his proposal to close the cow paths. Ten votes in favor, 9 against, Gérard gasped.

Well, this was simply not possible, because she, as one of the council members, had been absent from the vote, Adèle responded.

He was not clear on the details, he said, but apparently Debasse had invoked a little-known by-law which stated that if a council member had missed a certain number of sequential meetings... The end of Gérard's sentence was muddled into an incomprehensible slur as he fell forward onto a chair nearby.

Everyone in the room stared at each other in shock. Adèle placed her hand on her chest in a protective gesture. If her sickness had fused the days into weeks, this news brought her sharply back to reality. Beside her, Trouvert sat crestfallen. He had tried hard to oppose the mayor's plan, but his efforts had been in vain.

Adèle's blue eyes deepened, gathering the intense energy that Mathilde had come to recognize: it was like a ball of fire that sprung from within her, gaining speed, engulfing all that surrounded her. Adèle recalled acknowledging some benefits to closing the path during her earlier conversation with the mayor, but the fact that he had gone behind her back when she was at her most vulnerable confirmed his dishonest intentions. What a coward, she thought. She had really underestimated his wily ways.

Adèle clutched the armrest and rose to her feet. The first round had been lost, she admitted, turning to her guests. But this was only the beginning.

CHAPTER FIFTEEN

The next morning, Adèle rose early, galvanized by the events of the previous night. Despite Bernadine's disapproving look, she resumed her early walks through the countryside, bundling herself up in a large woolen coat. She went through the wooded vale and then back up through the orchard. A light morning frost laced the blades of grass in the fields. She marveled at the absence of fruit on the bare branches of the apple trees.

She had arranged to see Trouvert before Mass began, so rather than heading back home, she walked down to the village. All along, she had been confident that the motion would not be passed since the camp opposing the path's closure was fiercely entrenched. But it seemed that Debasse had found an underhanded way to go around her and rally the vote. The news had certainly shaken both Adèle and the priest, and the mayor's outrageous deed called for retaliation.

In the sacristy, Trouvert adjusted his dark cassock and surplice, smoothing out his well-pressed pleats. He glanced to the side at the festive chasuble kept in the closet for the special feast that would soon be upon them. For the past few weeks, he had worked tirelessly on the preparations for All Saints' Day.

But today, he was still reeling from what had happened the night before at the municipal council. Could they all not see that the path was the very life force that had served the land for centuries, connecting villages and families together for feasts and processions? It was Calignac's heart and soul, he exclaimed, the humid stillness of the sacristy as his only witness.

Gazing out the narrow window, he reflected on Debasse's numerous attempts over the years to gnaw away at the spiritual cornerstones of the village with the sole objective of furthering his personal ambitions. Debasse saw the church as a threat to his advancement and deliberately ignored the fact that in Calignac, faith, history, and traditions were inextricably intertwined. Using man's laws to manipulate and usurp heaven's designs was an insult to God's will. Ah… Ego, always *ego*, he grumbled with exasperation. He planned his sermon to decry this reckless project and the inequitable voting process by which it had been ratified.

As Adèle scuttled into the church, she heard her steps echo under its Romanesque vaults. Transverse rays of light radiated through the stained-glass windows; their diffraction fell on the heavy stone slabs and paved the floor, forming a multi-colored rosette that seemed to undulate like a vibrant wave of energy.

She paused, transported by this incandescent vision. The wave was pulling her in closer, gently circling around her and wrapping her like a woven cloth of light. A limitless feeling of expansion washed over her. Interior and exterior merged in a single flush as the gleaming floor disappeared under her feet. Chrysanthemums graced the pristine navel and chancel. These flowers of crimson—St. Calin's color—seemed to float around her as she reached the altar where she always stopped in front of a painting hung in the recess of one of the side apses. The work of Henri Martin, this painting that had been anonymously gifted to the parish decades ago. It depicted rows of tall, slender poplars tracing the curve of the Dordogne River, their pale leaves seemingly whispering in the breeze. Her eyes lingered on the scene as if to drink it in. The willows brushed softly the edge of the water as the wind toyed with them. Her eyes hovered over a yellow brushstroke that called her because it reminded her of a golden place, the golden place in her heart—her wooded vale. She contemplated this small world of beauty in a suspended moment of wistful longing. The chiming of the bells brought her back to reality. There was no time to lose.

When she put her head through the door, she found Trouvert kneeling in prayer with his long wooden rosary hanging from his waist. Hearing footsteps, he turned around. In the light of day, Adèle's drawn features made her face look so thin.

Had she not slept the previous night? he inquired in a caring yet reproachful tone.

She smiled back at his fatherly frown. Then, gently and without a word, he led her to the back of the sacristy, where he knew they could not be overheard. It was only then that Adèle noticed Trouvert's clenched jaw; in a quick flash, he reported what he had learned that morning. The vote had been that close, he demonstrated with his fingers almost touching, his voice full of pained restraint.

She would not believe what he had to tell her: the council's tenth vote had been none other than hers!

CHAPTER SIXTEEN

Parishioners streamed out of the church in a gloomy mood, still smarting from Trouvert's words. Passionately grasping the banister of the pulpit, the priest had warned them that closing down the path would equate to the repudiation of their faith, and hence the betrayal of St. Calin's spirit and dedication to good works.

Madame Sardelois had stayed behind to discuss the issue with Adèle and Trouvert. During Trouvert's sermon, it had become clear to her that someone needed to step up and intervene. She urged them to put their minds together to see what could be done in the short term to oppose the mayor's plans, which they agreed probably necessitated finding a candidate to run against him in the next elections. Obviously, Adèle's ill health and Trouvert's position in the clergy prevented either of them from running for office.

That left Madame Sardelois... Trouvert proposed, realizing the magnitude of what he was suggesting.

Madame Sardelois had shrugged her shoulders like a first grader attempting to avoid being summoned to the blackboard by the teacher. All her life, she had sought to raise Bruno and fade in the shadows of her own humility. Serving others in the background had been her way of overcoming her husband's tragic death, a means of alleviating the grief, the scars of which still ran deep.

But now, Trouvert was pleading with her to put aside her fear of public speaking in the interest of the common good. He reminded his devoted parishioner that she would not face this crisis alone; he and Adèle would be standing by her side.

Something had to be done to preserve Calignac's cultural and religious heritage, Adèle continued, placing her comforting hand on Madame Sardelois' shoulder. They could also count on Debasse's wife's unwavering support. Indeed, the gentle Constance had already staunchly opposed the closing, even apologizing for her husband's reckless decision.

ACROSS THE CHURCH SQUARE, a cohort of boisterous men had gathered at Brévin's to celebrate the mayor's victory. A savvy businessman, the merry café owner had a talent for *convivialité* and understood the commercial potential of these moments when a small circle of men got together to discuss village matters. He came out from behind his metal counter, holding a circular tray aloft.

Four coffees and a walnut liqueur! Brévin cheered. The *Boucher* was also in a gay mood. Standing up and patting Léonard on the shoulder, he announced that they were teaming up to capture the wild boar still at large in the woods. Raising their cups and glasses, the company chuckled in good spirits, cheerfully laughing and chortling at their reckless plan.

Suddenly the door opened and Debasse strutted into the room with a wide grin on his face. His supporters stared at him with sheeplike admiration as he walked towards the table. He delighted in these moments of glory. Taking this silence as an opportunity to salute the mayor's intervention, Didier reached for his glass and offered a toast to *the* man who had made it his priority to protect his cherished vineyard and Calignac from the threat of invasion. Those pilgrims and the scum that they brought with them were no more than rampaging hordes of dangerous drifters.

It was clear that Debasse's theory about poachers was gaining momentum. If few took the time to discuss the many unanswered questions surrounding the situation, many villagers feared that their properties would be adversely impacted. Yet, what everyone wanted to know at that moment was how Debasse had managed to push this agenda forward so quickly.

It came down to attention to details, the mayor

finished enigmatically, raising his index finger in the air for added dramatic effect.

Debasse knew full well that his plan had really hung by a thread until the last minute, and he was not about to tell the whole story. In fact, he had little if anything to do with this successful outcome. Adèle's absence for more than three council sessions required her vote to be counted in the affirmative. Under these highly unusual circumstances, the result of the vote had been 10 to 9, and the motion had therefore passed according to the provisions of the municipal law.

It had been that easy—but that close!

CHAPTER SEVENTEEN

That afternoon, Adèle took Mathilde's hand, bringing her into the study to resume their Sunday afternoon reflection time. They would sit by the fire and talk about life, about the small and big things that preoccupied the little girl. Recently, Adèle tried to broach the topic of some of life's paradoxes—ones that often eluded even adults.

Contrary to what one might think, discipline and good manners were not an impediment to life's pleasure, but rather the foundation for finding lasting pleasure and developing a sense of belonging with the world. They were the basic roadmap to deepen everyday experiences, nurturing the passion to learn, and fostering the desire to grow.

She realized that such notions were difficult for a child to grasp. But she had been heartened to notice a change in Mathilde, a subtle yet steadfast effort to make amends and to notice the needs of others. The betrayal and ache caused by the death of the fox had led the little girl to reflect in a way that she had not done before, and in doing so, had surely helped her to mature.

It was all a question of perspective, Adèle mused as she caught Mathilde's wide-eyed look. Of course, she knew Mathilde still wanted to saunter through the fields unfettered, but it was clear that she had turned a corner and was ready, more than ever before, to listen and to learn.

This time, in an unusual role reversal, Mathilde settled firmly into the large plush velvet armchair that made her feel like a miniature doll, while Bonne-Maman took the sofa. Adèle had sat back, for a moment, delighting in her grandchild's heart-shaped face that stared back at her full of spirit and quiet resolve.

Did Mathilde remember their conversation from a few weeks back? Adèle asked after moments of silence. There was something kind and gentle in her grandmother's voice, like the summer breeze coming up from the valley to stroke her cheeks.

Did Mathilde remember the magical moments she had spent watching her furry friend? Did she recall the first time she had even laid eyes on it? Bonne-Maman continued. Yes, the first time Mathilde had spotted the fox, she had spent the afternoon skipping through Finoud's fragrant alfalfa fields looking for the perfect freckled toad as the sun came down over the valley, beyond the tall poplars... Adèle let those last words linger on her tongue, and then carried on softly.

Was it not the same joy she felt when she bit into one of Bernadine's butter biscuits, or stretched out her cold little feet towards the scorching hearth on winter nights? Bonne-Maman questioned as if privy to all of Mathilde's dreamy thoughts. There were so many of these small and special moments, Adèle remarked, weren't there? What did these moments all have in common?

Mathilde was not quite sure how to respond.

After a few long minutes, the elder woman took Mathilde's hand and slowly led her to the French doors that overlooked the wooded vale. Yes, we belong to the earth, she said, this one stretching below—the one that saw us take our first steps, watched over us, guiding the course of our lives and our happiness. People were curiously like oak trees with deep roots penetrating the soil that supported them, leaves enriching the air they breathed and spirits soaring high towards the sky, Adèle went on in a dreamy voice.

This land had always been at the core of her grandmother, who, as a small child, tottered valiantly around the stone terrace. The vista had been no more than a twinkle, a flash in the distance, something that she glimpsed from time to time.

Mathilde too belonged to this land; in fact, she did not yet know it, but one day, it would be part and parcel of her entire being. The connection was there, lying in wait—it just needed to be awakened. Pain often did that for us. Pain was a precious guide; all Mathilde had to do was listen to the Guide, the whispers that would lead her to see the path. This earth was all that mattered: one had to love it because it had made us, it was in us, it *was* us, she finished.

Their eyes gazed at the wooded vale, and it seemed that for the very first time, Mathilde felt its mysterious and opaque attraction shimmering below, as dusk greeted the freckled night.

CHAPTER EIGHTEEN

The next morning, Mathilde was awakened by tumultuous activity downstairs. Stumbling out of bed, she rushed barefoot to the top of the stairs and leaned on the balustrade. Bonne-Maman and Bernadine were making winter preparations both inside and outside. At least for now, the chain of command had been restored to its rightful order; Gérard had come out of his hibernation and Bernadine followed Adèle's orders with a sense of immeasurable relief and genuine enjoyment.

Bernadine had climbed atop a stool and was hanging the heavily lined tapestry curtains that Adèle had sewn the winter before. Adèle stood near the stool, lifting the curtain little by little to facilitate the installation. Together they were a remarkable team: what Bernadine lacked in ideas, Adèle compensated for with her keen and resourceful *savoir-faire* in all areas of daily life.

The past month had been trying for Adèle's health and she relished every positive sign that refuted the *Docteur*'s diagnosis. Winter was coming, though. Heating these thick stone walls always proved a challenge, even with three fireplaces and a wood-burning stove in the kitchen. Adèle did not fear the cold so much as the dampness that seemed to seep through the walls during these harsh months—especially the ones to come.

Debasse had long awaited this morning. Standing in his entrance foyer, facing a gilded mirror, he obsessively re-tied the knot of his tie. Heavy silk never seemed to go his way, he grumbled. Never mind that over the last few days, his wife Constance had been strangely silent. He could only guess that she was distressed by the vote about the Pilgrims' Path. Although her allegiance to Trouvert was no secret, he had to admit that he had underestimated her religious devotion when they had first married. Since then, not a day passed when he did not fear that her faith might stand in the way of his ambitions. But he would manage, as he always did.

He was preparing to head out to the station to welcome his great friend Courteline, the Parisian. He had met Courteline during a memorable trip to Paris and instantly felt they were kindred spirits, though he sometimes suspected the feeling was one-sided. For once, his relentless ambition—something that locals could not fathom —had found the perfect partnership in Courteline's unabashed narcissism. The festivities of the *Fête de la Truffe* were the perfect occasion to discuss his business plan with the Parisian *restaurateur*.

The tie finally fell in place, and he stared one more time at his reflection with great satisfaction. He checked the time again. The *Bouchère* had requested an appointment to finalize the last details of the fair, but she would have to wait. He smoothed his close-shaven mustache and headed for the door. He could not wait to bask once again in the aura of sophistication that always surrounded the Parisian.

On the train to Calignac, Courteline stared out the window. A former Michelin gourmet expert, he had recently opened his own restaurant in Paris. Its theme was traditional dishes from the *Quercy* region complete with authentic and impeccably fresh produce—whether game, vegetables, or herbs—everything was imported directly from the region. This past year, the accolades in the *Gault et Millau* for his promotion of *Quercy cuisine* had given him much satisfaction. But his success came at a price: the constant feeling of uncertainty related to finding a dependable supply from this primitive region. Even a short lapse could mean disaster for a restaurant that operated daily.

This vulnerability was an acute source of stress in his daily life, a nagging reminder that compelled him to visit the region personally on a regular basis. He had left Paris earlier that morning with his friend Turgot and embarked on this long and circuitous journey that cut through the whole of France, north to south. He could not help but lament how Calignac was in the middle of nowhere, and it seemed that returning there grew more and more tedious with every trip. Yet he hoped that this time, he would come closer to achieving his aims.

Sitting across from him, his friend Turgot had dozed off, with his head bobbing from side to side with each bend of the train tracks. An antique specialist, he spent all of his waking hours hunched over the arcane complications of tourbillon watches. In fact, it was only a few months ago, after years of resistance, that Turgot had finally given in and agreed to come along with his friend, his curiosity piqued by the tales he kept hearing about this uncivilized region with its exquisite *cuisine*.

Still another half hour to go, he grumbled to himself, staring at Turgot's complacently naive face. The country-side stretched seamlessly, with barely a trace of civilization. How would his lanky companion cope without his downy mattress and his nightly gardenia tuberose–scented bath ritual? He feared that Turgot was in for a rude awakening. Rows of verdant poplars caught the sun in a constant play of light and shade as the train progressed. Turgot suddenly jerked awake, blinking at the strong sun glaring through the windows.

Did this not feel like the far edge of the world? Courteline prompted, as he pointed at the Dordogne cliffs speckled with dark holes.

The entrance to caves? Turgot exclaimed with excitement. He could not help but jabber about the Lascaux

Caves that he had recently discovered in the newspaper *Carrefour*. An exceptional Paleolithic series of galleries, containing numerous impressive paintings of deer, aurochs, ibex, bison, horses, and bears, the work of the first modern humans, *Homo Sapiens*, 17,000 years ago.

Unfortunately, this incomparable site was now being threatened by a dearth of oxygen. There was talk of a mysterious algae—what some scientists called a microscopic mushroom—slowly eroding the walls as throngs of visitors streamed through the galleries, causing the atmospheric conditions to change and thus altering the thermic balance that had, until now, allowed these marvels to be preserved intact.

Did Courteline know that leading experts from the *Musée du Louvre* had made the trip to the region to authenticate this prodigious discovery? Would they be able to reverse the degradation of these unique drawings? Turgot jabbered on excitedly. But Courteline had stopped listening to Turgot's rambling.

Instead, he nodded absently. He was adept at dismissing anything that was not directly related to his desires. When visiting Calignac the previous year, he had inquired about going on a truffle hunt with one of the locals, but his insistent requests were bluntly denied. This just increased his determination. He knew that the whereabouts of truffles was considered sacred knowledge; it was not a tour that just anyone could join—but he was Courteline, after all, and he demanded access.

The *Fête de la Truffe*, yes, that was all that mattered to him, he thought, cocking his head to one side with aloofness.

CHAPTER NINETEEN

On the platform, poised and proud, Debasse could hardly contain his impatience. He peered in the distance beyond the aqueduct. Of course, it was not the first time they met but Debasse was convinced that this encounter with Courteline would determine his future. For this occasion, he had taken care in hand-picking the welcome committee, which included most of the town *commerçants*, Brévin, the *Boucher*, and the *Boulanger*, but also a few members of the municipal council. The mayor had cautioned the committee about the crucial roles each of them played in placing Calignac on the map.

A whistle resounded in the clear air and soon a large black locomotive rumbled into the station. Sluggishly, it came to a long screeching halt in a cloud of smoke. The platform was inundated by a crowd of travelers, families parting, rejoining, waving hands and drying teary eyes.

Debasse searched the crowd anxiously and finally made out the two Parisians slowly emerging from the bustle.

Even after their long and exhausting journey, they stepped down from the car, dressed impeccably, surrounded by a myriad of crocodile-leather suitcases and hat boxes that the train conductor had kindly gathered for them. Debasse immediately rushed to Courteline and seized upon his gloved hand effusively. Then he turned to Léonard and motioned him to handle his guests' travel bags. Neither Courteline nor Turgot budged, fully expecting to be assisted.

As he started walking along the platform, Turgot looked around, lost in a daze. He was assaulted by all the sensory stimuli. The *Boucher*, the *Boulanger*, and Brévin were commenting loudly on the improvements in the recent technology of trains, while the dark and unkempt Léonard lagged behind, sweating under the weight of the mountain of luggage that had been pushed on him. The hunter stopped for a minute to wipe his brow and then spat on the train tracks with relish. Haggard from his trip, Turgot seriously wondered how Courteline had befriended such uncouth and coarse company. He had never encountered such people —people who spoke loudly, breathed heavily, and smelled so pungently.

From the sidelines, the elders observed the scene. Although they usually spent their days under the old lime tree on the village square, they had decided to relocate for that special occasion. Comfortably seated in the shade, they would not have missed this sight, which, in their opinion, deserved much comment.

Parisians were a species of their own. These people scoffed at their coarseness and eschewed their talents; yet, ironically enough, they had no quandary invading these very regions during the summer holidays. Parisians leeched on *Quercy's* rich gastronomy, pretending to know it all. They always came with a particular air of self-entitlement, which rubbed locals the wrong way. The elders poked fun at the fact that, despite these impatient Parisians who demanded service "their way," Calignac had not changed for centuries and would always outlast any outside influence.

As the station was a short walk to town, the mayor had not arranged any other type of transportation. Turgot huffed and puffed, wondering how long of a trek this would be while Courteline walked at the head of the troupe with Debasse. The mayor showered the Parisian with compliments while enjoying his own elaborate explanations of town monuments.

As they passed through the Romanesque archway—remains of the medieval ramparts that once fortified the village—Debasse silently congratulated himself on how well he had planned this visit. He had Courteline exactly where he wanted him, he thought. Soon Parisians, villagers, and regional pilgrims would witness the magnificence of the *Fête de la Truffe* and testify to his visionary leadership as mayor.

But as they progressed through the narrow village

streets, Debasse perceived cautious appreciation on the villagers' faces—or was it apprehension? His infatuation with himself often blinded him. He knew he was not universally liked and that many resented him for closing the path and compromising the cultural way of life of the *terroir* they cherished. Debasse cycled through the different possibilities as he tried to interpret the uneasy atmosphere that he had detected upon entering the village. He figured that it was just nerves, the excitement and the pressure mounting with Courteline's arrival.

As they reached the town square, they caught sight of an unusual gathering around the fountain of St. Calin. Why was everyone staring at the basin? Could it be that the villagers had finally understood the importance of Courteline's arrival and rallied to support their mayor's initiative? As they got closer though, he started to make out something entirely different. Montrelazet, the *Docteur*, was gesticulating about while Alavert, the *Pharmacien*, stood to the side, leaning over the fountain with a puzzled look. He also spotted Trouvert hurrying across the square intrigued by the tumult outside.

Suddenly, the *Bouchère* erupted from the crowd and yanked him by the arm. Debasse had to see this for himself, she cried with alarm. Dismissively, he forged ahead.

As he reached the edge, everyone stared back at him, and he knew something cataclysmic had happened. He stared at the polygonal basin, incredulous. Despite his best efforts to remain calm, his stomach began churning with agitation. The basin water had turned bright red, like blood. Crimson water, they all muttered anxiously, as if to echo his horror. And it was not just the basin that was filled with red water. At the top of the fountain, surmounted by the statue of St. Calin, rose a pier featuring four spouts and out of each one gushed the same crimson liquid.

Sacré bleu—bloody hell—what was happening? Things were falling apart.

CHAPTER TWENTY

Over the following days, the fountain water showed no sign of clearing. Every morning at dawn, Debasse rushed across the square to check in with Alavert, the *Pharmacien*. He would have to put his fate in the hands of science. Alavert would run his tests and come up with a solution, for sure. Why was this happening to him, just when he was about to see his deepest desires come to fruition? Why now with the *Fête de la Truffe* so close? This bloody color simply had to disappear, Debasse growled to himself. But day after day, Debasse's disappointment and fears only grew.

The water remained scarlet. What discouraged Alavert most was that because the actual source of the spring had always remained a mystery, there was no way of tracing the water to its origin. St. Calin's water had always seemed to gush miraculously from the depths of the earth. Curiously, there had been no reported deaths of livestock in the valley since the color had changed. However, the pungent smell, which had worsened over the past days, was most disconcerting, he thought, meticulously charting out calculations in his notebook.

Cautious not to disturb Alavert in his work, villagers sensed the gravity of the situation. When the *Pharmacien* retreated to his office to clear his mind, they gathered around the polygonal basin to debate and lament the scourge that now tainted the village's good fortune. Was the Saint punishing them for something they had done or left undone? Maybe this was a warning against the closing of the path, and this was Calin's way of expressing his discontentment? In any case, each had a different interpretation of the phenomenon, and they bickered over the different shades of red that the water seemed to take on, depending on the hour of the day. Mornings and evenings sent forth the darkest hue. Was it vermilion, maroon, cherry red, or simply blood red? Everyone argued and wanted to be right.

Alavert and Montrelazet were less concerned about the color and more worried about potential contamination. Indeed, although villagers had municipal water piped into their homes, many washed their hands or regularly took sips from the fountain, while others still believed in its therapeutic virtues

Public health being of paramount importance, they insisted unanimously that no one drink from it. Only tap water was to be drunk, preferably boiled. As a result, villagers flocked to the pharmacy, the only place that sold bottled water, Vittel and Évian, but supplies were already running out. Montrelazet was also overwhelmed with extra appointments for patients who were convinced of mysterious or imaginary symptoms.

As the news spread fast to neighboring villages, not only had farmers stopped taking their flocks to nearby streams, but the flow of daily pilgrims had skyrocketed overnight. For centuries, pilgrims had traveled to Calignac out of devotion to the Saint who healed ulcers and other skin ailments with the miraculous water. And now they wanted to see this extraordinary phenomenon for themselves.

From the sidelines, the two Parisians witnessed the turmoil that had seized Calignac. They listened to all their opinions, amused and entertained. Many villagers now felt that they needed to rectify any wandering from the original spirit of the village. These themes of morality reminded the two snobs of the comic operas they enjoyed on warm summer nights at the *Palais Garnier.*

Although he failed to make any breakthrough, the *Pharmacien* could not help but notice that the color was inexplicably fading as days passed. He started to speculate that it might be connected to the recent rains. This new development was both a curse and a blessing, he thought, scratching his chin. Soon there would be little to no red water left to do a proper test. His chances of solving the mystery and preventing a recurrence were slipping away.

By Friday morning, Debasse strolled over for an update. All night, he had been tossing and turning in his large canopy bed, praying—as much as his lack of faith would allow—to find the water transparent again. And there it was, right in front of him! The stream had become completely clear again and crystalline water was now splashing into the fountain's basin.

Debasse beamed with contentment: his worries had simply washed away—literally! Alavert returned Debasse's sanguine smile with a dubious frown. As a man of science, the *Pharmacien* was frustrated because things still made no sense. He could not guarantee the red water would not return, but Debasse did not care in the least. Things had returned to normal, and that was all that mattered.

The *Fête de la Truffe* was a week away and no long-dead Saint would rob him of the success that he deserved.

CHAPTER TWENTY-ONE

The following afternoon, Courteline knocked on Adèle's imposing oak entry door. He checked his hands, for he could not bear the thought of appearing in public with less than perfect fingernails. He intended to get himself invited to the famous *Soirée des petits fours* that Adèle hosted following the *Fête de la Truffe*.

Ushered by Bernadine into the study, Courteline found Adèle engrossed in a manual of botany, Mathilde at her side.

They had been learning the virtues and dangers of *Digitalis*, commonly known as foxglove, Adèle explained as a form of greeting. Botany was one of her passions, and she and Mathilde had begun exploring a new plant every week, she continued.

Did Courteline know that a few drops of digitalis could be used as an effective cardiac stimulant, while too many could cause heart failure?

He nodded politely, dismissing this information that was of no interest to him. He sat opposite Adèle on the velvet sofa. Once settled against the plush pillows, he turned around, his nostrils flaring wide: something succulent was within reach. Emerging from the corridor, Bernadine entered with her famous golden-crusted walnut caramel *tarte* in her hands. He had been scheming to steal her recipe for a while, but his attempts had been in vain.

Across the coffee table, coiled like a cat, Mathilde stared at this unusual man with keen interest. Adèle crossed her legs, amused; she could only guess what was going through her granddaughter's head. She remembered when she was young and first confronted by the theatrics of such a rarefied creature. Courteline was a prime example of a self-absorbed city dweller, with his affected mannerisms and speech. This would be interesting. His visit was a unique opportunity for Mathilde to gain insight into human nature.

Adèle sat with elegant ease, watching this self-deluded socialite as he tried to engage tastefully in conversation. Adèle's slender hands started playing with her long strand of pearls.

Was the country air not delightfully refreshing today? he finally asked.

Mathilde had been studying the large rug, and it struck her that adult conversations bore a likeness to the meandering lines that her eyes traced along the intricate and colorful patterns before her. They often curved and turned, but always circled back to their original impetus. Mathilde was tickled to recognize the Parisian's unsubtle *entrée en matière*—the broaching of a delicate subject—and her little dimples creased with pleasure at the corners of her cheekbones.

Yes, no doubt, and there was nothing better for one's health than a forced stay in the country, Adèle replied playfully. He nodded, irritated at the mention of these provincial benefits.

He was in town until the *Fête de la Truffe* and would gladly join in the celebration she was hosting that Sunday, were she kind enough to extend the invitation to himself, an outsider.

She had expected his request and acquiesced to his feigned deference. Adèle had a reputation for her patience, but such forced and tedious meetings tended to irk her, especially when she could predict the outcome of the conversation.

Courteline's front teeth sank greedily into the succulent treat. Although he was on his third slice, he still could not identify the *tarte's* ingredients. As his mouth filled with the buttery-salty flavor of the roasted walnuts, his voracious consumption betrayed a momentary lack of refinement. Mathilde tilted her head, cupping her hand under her chin, and peered at him with an inquisitive look. There was something crude about him, animal-like, beneath the veneer, Mathilde thought.

Courteline emerged from his gastronomic trance. He

seemed to draw a blank for a minute, suddenly startled by the little girl's inquisitive stare.

CHAPTER TWENTY-TWO

Then Courteline sat up, leaning forward as if to make a confession. In truth, he had come to Calignac with the hope of wrapping up his business with Debasse.

Business with the mayor? Adèle asked with seeming indifference although Mathilde had registered a nearly imperceptible twitch of her upper lip.

Yes, he went on, his restaurant in Paris required a solid supplier of the region's best ingredients and meats, and Debasse had offered to support the expansion of his business. Parisians wanted to experience authentic *Quercy cuisine* and direct shipments from the Dordogne were the only way to guarantee quality, freshness, and quantity. Courteline paused, tickled to see that he had Adèle's attention.

That evening he would attend a private banquet that the mayor was hosting in his honor—a fantastic occasion to discuss plans with local merchants, suppliers, and wholesalers, he continued. Yes, Debasse had a keen eye for opportunities, Adèle agreed as she reached behind her to poke the smoldering embers.

But to be honest, he had one unfulfilled dream… truffles… Courteline let out a sigh, looking at Mathilde and Adèle in turn. Yes, nothing compared to the taste of black truffles, he mused, taking another bite of the *tarte*. Unfortunately, in recent decades, truffle supply had drastically dwindled. In fact, for the past few days, he had been scouring the region to locate people who knew how to improve the odds of farming truffles. Indeed, he intended to revolutionize the gourmet scene and make truffles available to Parisians. He was eager to hear Adèle's opinion on the topic. Had she ever heard of truffles being deliberately cultivated? he inquired through another mouthful.

Adèle seemed to ponder his request for a minute. She caught Mathilde's puzzled look and winked at her out of the corner of her eye.

Yes, truffles were a mystery to them all, Adèle carried on with an enigmatic smile, apparently indulging his inquiry despite his tactlessness. To be fair, she could only recount the stories she had heard others tell. For example, years ago, a mature journeyman had passed through the village, claiming to grow truffles on demand. These promises might have been enthralling elsewhere, but in Calignac they were met with skepticism, or at least, amused silence. The salesman had stood proud and tall on market days, loudly advertising the little booklet detailing his scientific methods—along with a kit he sold which contained the secrets to producing truffles. But very quickly, it became obvious that he was appealing to the wrong crowd.

What had become of the salesman? What about the manual? Courteline asked with a greed he could hardly conceal. He had vanished mysteriously without a word, Adèle replied, aware of the spellbinding power of her story, not only for Courteline but also for her grandchild. But if farming truffles was an impossible enterprise, finding them *was* possible, given, of course, a certain talent and flair, Adèle went on. Truffles were unlike any other fungus, for they were the magnificent and mysterious result of Nature's capricious genius and man's *savoir-faire*. Truffles did not linger exclusively on oak tree roots; sometimes they settled in the mesh of hazelnut tree roots. In any case, truffles always chose the tree, the land, and the *rabassier*—the truffle expert. That is, the truffle seeker found favor with the truffle—not the other way around.

Adèle became more animated as she continued to unveil more about the topic close to her heart. One could neither expect to find them nor desire them too vainly. They required an absolute devotion to the earth and filled any seeker with deep humility. Even with a promising *trufferie*—a truffle-oak tree field—one silently hoped that after a few years of dedication and hard work, prayers might be answered: the mysterious truffle mycelium would elect to light on the root system of one or even several trees. Early on, children in the region were trained to watch for the signs of such favor, Adèle finished, noticing with satisfaction that Courteline glanced sideways at Mathilde.

The little girl whom he had dismissed early on might not be as insignificant after all.

CHAPTER TWENTY-THREE

As soon as Courteline departed, Adèle closed her eyes and considered her unsettled feeling at the mention of Debasse. She remained with the discomfort until it sank in, slowly, seeping into the pores of her diaphanous skin, until it traveled far within, following the coils of her being to reach the center, her very core. There it grew bigger, wider, churning and expanding to the outer limits, the extremities of her fingers. They tingled warmly. Suddenly her eyes reopened as a thought flashed through her mind.

Could it be...? She could not wait a minute longer. She had to check.

Leaving Mathilde behind with a pile of homework, Adèle headed down to the vale.

The air was brisk. After a few days of respite, the cold had returned and the frost reappeared, with its biting white lace adorning the bushes and trees. Her boots effortlessly guided her past the naked fruit trees of the orchard, their bare arms stretched to the sky in worship. They looked so desolate yet serene in the winter, she mused, as they awaited the transformation of spring. Gérard had finally gotten around to cutting back the thorny hedge. The day was ending, and the sun rested on the horizon, orange and solemn. The rays guided her over the stony wall into the vale.

Everything was quiet except for a few sparrows hunting for meager sustenance.

Pushing aside dry brambles, she entered a clearing covered with small dry stones. In the center stood four short scrawny oak trees with their tortured and knotted silhouettes low to the ground. Memories of playing hide-and-seek in the vale flooded her mind and she remembered taking refuge behind their split barked bodies to elude her friends' search.

She paused for an instant. Then her steps instinctively guided her back towards a shepherd's shelter, built against the side of a cliff, that stood deeper in the vale, concealed behind screens of ivy and boxwood. Each stone held fast without any mortar by virtue of its perfect shape and angle, thanks to the skill of a nameless shepherd from long ago. But one stone in particular protruded from the cliff wall, and because of its location, it had always been the ideal place to hang game.

As she approached, something caught her attention. The flat stone that normally lay across the threshold of the entrance had been moved. Bending forward, she entered the tight space and was suddenly overwhelmed by the very familiar smell of fresh blood. After her eyes adjusted to the darkness, she eventually spotted a large burlap bag tucked behind the entrance wall. She quickly loosened the strings, and as her hand reached inside, her fingers encountered something unmistakably warm and viscous.

As she removed her hand, she glimpsed the dark maroon stain on her fingertips, and a shiver of disgust washed over her. It was like a flash, a blinding current that ran through her shoulders, along her spine, a force that compelled her to reach inside once more. This time, she pulled out lifeless quails, pheasants, hares, and even a small wild boar. Shiny black eyes still vibrant with life stared back at Adèle in the gloom and, in a blink, conjured up the image of the little pheasant on the *Bouchère*'s stall.

For a moment, her gaze became disoriented by the intensity of the fading blue landscape beyond the open door. When she refocused on her surroundings, she was horrified to make out still more dead pheasants, all hanging by a string wound around the shelter's roof. All the pieces of the puzzle fell into place: the closing of the Pilgrims' Path, the mayor's insistent visit, this bag of poached animals in the shelter, the ambitious Courteline's arrival for the *Fête de la Truffe*—what a dreadful discovery this all was!

She shuddered. Her worst nightmare had come true. It was now plainly obvious that her contrived contamination of the fountain had not been enough to stop Debasse in his tracks. Now, the pressure was mounting, and she would have to take her resourcefulness to the next level. Of course, that would only be possible if... *Oh, mon Dieu...*

After searching for a while, she spotted a host of plants with four narrow greenish threadlike leaves arranged in opposing pairs. Kneeling, she carefully gathered a handful of purple berries, their deep, lustrous hues glistening against the muted greens of the underwood. Wasting no time, she went back into the shelter, and her slender hands quickly went to work, crushing a berry in each animal's mouth. Suddenly, she froze.

There was a faint noise in the distance. She quickly pressed her body against the wall. She barely had time to release the strings of the bag before a large, powerful hand reached into the shelter and grabbed it from the other side. She could still hear the heavy breathing of the man as he grumbled a few words in *patois*, the local dialect. Whoever he was, he knew his way around, and he had not even bothered to step in. Still in shock, Adèle stayed crouched in the shelter for several long minutes.

When she finally headed home, she did not know that two sharp eyes were watching her.

CHAPTER TWENTY-FOUR

In the winter evening, Debasse's house gleamed in the distance like a faceted jewel. Debasse and Courteline had been engrossed in conversation, reviewing the details of their future trade and defining the exact terms of the agreement: standards of quality, frequency, delivery, and profit margins.

Courteline could not believe that they had come this far in such a short time. Although he still did not trust the mayor completely. Such quantities were staggering, thought the Parisian, torn between skepticism and greed. Yet, he could already picture himself as the talk of every Parisian *salon*, his name on everyone's lips. Socialites and aristocrats would vie for his presence in their inner circles, he mused.

With circumspection, they continued their negotiation. Substantial personal risks were involved for Debasse if anything went awry. So, he would want a substantial financial guarantee and an agreement in writing.

For Courteline, much less was at stake although his reputation was not nothing. Of course, if Debasse failed to perform his portion of the contract, there would be late fees or penalties for defective or damaged goods. His business in Paris depended on smooth supply so he wanted to be certain that Debasse would deliver on his promise. Finally, since the game was procured illicitly, the contract would naturally have to remain confidential.

Were they not gentlemen and men of honor after all? Debasse asked with a chuckle.

They raised their glasses to seal the agreement and glanced at each other with the same conniving gleam. Exhilarated by his sense of accomplishment, Debasse could not refrain from patting his new partner on the shoulder. The Parisian managed to suppress his disdain for his interlocutor's smarmy collegiality.

This milestone called for a celebration over a sump-tuous dinner, Debasse said, motioning to his guest. He had invited a few personalities hand-picked from the surrounding villages. Their help could prove crucial, the mayor added with a cunning smile. The two men glided across the parquet under the imposing chandelier that lit the foyer. They entered the dining room where an elegant table had been set with *Limoges* plates and *Baccarat* goblets glistening on a fine crisp linen tablecloth. Debasse had promised a spectacular feast, and Courteline's eyes widened, momentarily revealing his excitement as he sat down opposite Debasse at the end of the long table.

The soft chatter brushed against the fabric walls of the elegant room as the guests greeted each other. The light was dim and soft; the solemn butler entered, carrying the first dish. The wafting fragrances were divine, and Debasse was pleased to notice expressions of surprise and desire. The evening unfolded like a play, with each scene marked by the *dégustation* of exquisite courses. Debasse could finally relax, satisfied that things were finally coming together for him, right in time for the *Fête de la Truffe*.

In the chilly hours of the morning, someone knocked on Montrelazet's front door. Who could it be? A sleepy Montrelazet appeared on the doorstep, wearing his nightcap and gown. What was the matter? Could this not wait for his regular office hours? Rubbing his eyes, he squinted, and recognized Debasse's butler. Debasse was sending for him.

Constance had experienced another relapse? the *Docteur* asked with concern.

No, it was *Monsieur,* the mayor. He was not feeling well—it was extremely urgent.

Scrambling, Montrelazet changed from his flannel pajamas into a dark suit, reached for his spectacles and, grabbing his physician's leather bag, followed the butler into the night.

CHAPTER TWENTY-FIVE

Debasse struggled to reach for the basin that his wife had placed on his nightstand the previous night. The pressure contorting his bowels was intense and painful. After a rough sleepless night, rays of light darted through the shutters. What bug had he caught? Ahhaaa, he moaned in pain. And to think that the *Fête de la Truffe* was only four days away!

The timing could not be worse, he groaned pitifully, appealing to Constance. But she said nothing, her back to the burning chimney. He winced. She gazed back at him with the soft yet uncompromising look that she gave when he overstepped the boundaries she deemed appropriate.

At that moment, Montrelazet walked in with his leather attaché. During his nighttime visit, he had prescribed a few drops of medication. One glance at the patient told him that they had had no effect on what appeared to be a bad case of indigestion. Montrelazet decided to start from scratch. He noted the mayor's physical signs: fatigue, pale complexion, swollen abdomen, and throat. The *Docteur* pulled out his watch and took the patient's pulse. Low-grade fever, he concluded in a detached tone. So why had these drops not helped?

He opened his leather bag and pulled out his stethoscope. He needed to check the patient's chest again. Asking Debasse to cough loudly, Montrelazet made his way gradually from the man's back around to his chest and his rib cage. It was then that he noticed something peculiar: Debasse's belly was covered with an ugly red rash.

Although Montrelazet had seen a lot in his professional career, these target-shaped rings struck him as particularly odd. An infection? Impossible, he mumbled, his bedside manner momentarily lapsing as he could not disguise the intellectual curiosity triggered by such a strange sight.

Debasse was silent, transfixed by his speckled rolls of fat, while Montrelazet paced up and down the room with agitation. He remembered studying a range of skin diseases and infections in medical manuals, but had never actually witnessed anything of the sort.

Montrelazet questioned the patient again: Whom had he been in contact with? What on earth had he eaten in the last few days? Well, he already knew the answer; Debasse had just given him a full account the night before. Although the case did resemble classic indigestion in some ways, the additional symptoms—namely, the unsightly rash—were cause for concern. He would come back after consulting his reference manuals and case studies.

The mayor sank back beneath the covers, thinking of the *Fête de la Truffe* and the speech he had honed for weeks, the one he planned to give at the opening festivities. Why was this happening to him? Of course, he trusted the *Docteur*'s judgment. If anyone could get him well in time for Saturday, it was Montrelazet.

The *Docteur* grabbed his leather *trousse* and hat and turned to Constance. Debasse's vital signs were not alarming, he explained, but he wanted to be cautious and feared a possible contagion. The mayor was housebound, no visits under any circumstances. She would need to wash her hands regularly and was not to spoon feed him, even if he pleaded. Debasse was always playing for sympathy; Constance would have to stay firm at least until Montrelazet figured out what was happening.

The mayor's condition was an intriguing medical case, and Montrelazet hated to admit that this new development was giving him more of a thrill than the mystery of the fountain water, which had been Alavert's case. *His* life's mission was to solve medical enigmas. He remembered the passion he had felt during his residency, when his attendings brought forward cases impossible to diagnose. So many years ago, he reminisced with nostalgia.

As he stepped outside, the clattering of hammers against wood brought him back to reality. The preparations for the

Fête de la Truffe were almost finished. Near the church, men had unpacked the white canvas tent that would be hoisted atop the stage for the truffle contest. Vivid decorations hung on the wrought iron streetlamps, and the streets themselves were lined with colorful banners. In just four days, the village would begin filling up with bustling crowds of gawkers.

But it was unlikely that Debasse would be well enough to deliver his speech, Montrelazet admitted to himself. He wanted to be optimistic, but the reality was that this type of rash would take days to disappear. Although his patient exhibited no other abnormal signs, it was hard to say if the rash pointed to a more systemic infection that had not yet fully manifested itself. Time would tell, he mused, passing St. Calin's fountain.

Once home, Montrelazet steeped himself in volumes of anatomy, epidemiology, and virology. He entertained the premise that Debasse was suffering from an infectious disease. He then set off to work laboriously on two different experimental treatments in the hope of mitigating his patient's side effects. By early evening, he was back at the mayor's house. He climbed the stairs with eagerness. But when the door opened to reveal Debasse, Montrelazet could not help but gasp.

His watchful eyes scanned Debasse's body, baffled by the speed at which the rash had spread: the mayor's body was entirely covered with red spots. Debasse greeted him with a snarl. His whole body was itchy, and he was going out of his mind. He felt as if he were trapped in a cage and the burning sensation was unbearable. He motioned for the *Docteur* to come closer.

Had Montrelazet found the miracle cure yet? He could not stand staying inside any longer—he needed fresh air, he wanted to see his friends, he begged. But Montrelazet's response was firm. Leaving his bed was out of the question. He was to be quarantined, Montrelazet declared. Debasse looked at him with exasperation, and leaning over towards the *Docteur*, he reached for Montrelazet's arm. Avoiding the mayor's touch, Montrelazet moved a chair towards the bed and politely maintained his distance. He was listening.

Nobody could find out about this misfortune, Debasse pleaded in a whisper. Montrelazet nodded in assent. He had kept many more secrets over the years. The town was full of them. If people only knew.

A couple of days passed with no real sign of progress —albeit no further deterioration either. Montrelazet could not stand keeping this excitement to himself so in confidence, he finally came to share the details of this unusual story with his friend Alavert. They racked their brains over several cups of boiled coffee, throwing around ideas about a possible diagnosis. Yet, they came up empty-handed, irritated at their inability to solve the case. In the end, Alavert teased his colleague that there was only one thing that Debasse' rash reminded him of: the skin condition that St. Calin was said to have cured centuries ago! That legend was, of course, hearsay, but still, the similarities were ironic considering Debasse's disrespect for Calin's legacy.

Meanwhile, confined to his room, Debasse paced back and forth, unable to sit still. If the itch was now almost entirely gone, he was still covered with hundreds of ring-shaped spots all over his body. He was losing his mind and time was running out!

CHAPTER TWENTY-SIX

With preparations in full swing, Debasse's sudden absence from the village scene was all the more blatant. It was strange that the man who monitored every detail of the event— hovering over merchants and personally greeting all attendees—was simply nowhere to be found. Villagers first rumored that he was bedridden with a bad case of the flu, but they were now starting to speculate that things were more serious. No one knew anything, and the lack of information provided endless fodder for the folk who enjoyed gossip.

To the *Bouchère*, Debasse's absence was a disaster. She was bursting at the seams under pressure. She had gotten out of bed that morning at a ridiculously early hour to supervise the building of the stage where the contestants would stand before the jury, in hopes of being awarded the grand prize. She stretched a long rope to create a large perimeter around the stage to dissuade curious eyes from staring at the jury. She ordered Brévin to sweep up in front of his café—she wanted the area as clean and inviting as possible.

The commotion was making her wish she could return to chopping large pieces of meat with her steel cleaver or trimming large strands of fat. So, when Montrelazet walked through the square, she rushed toward him with frantic gestures. Where on earth was Debasse? Would she be forced to manage the logistics of the fair on her own—perhaps even addressing the crowd?

But the *Docteur* did not give a direct answer and brushed her aside. She could not imagine that Montrelazet's caution arose from a fear of contagion although in the last few days, the *Docteur* was reassured that Constance had not developed any symptoms.

Meanwhile, Finoud chatted with the cheerful *Boulangère* about the bounties of the village. What caliber of truffles would be entered in the contest this year? she asked. The previous year, the vineyard owner, Didier, had won first prize for an amazingly fragrant truffle, which had been the result of a fortuitous discovery that occurred when he was trimming his vines. Didier had been blessed that year with a velvety, spicy *cuvée*—and with even more good fortune. What a marvelous coincidence this had been!

Maybe this year, someone would uncover another

remarkable specimen, she speculated with enthusiasm, although it was unlikely to be Didier. Everyone knew that his vineyard had been compromised by the vagrants, the *Boulangère* finished as she wished Finoud a good day. She continued to arrange her shop window to create an attractive display. The aesthetic would have to be striking to catch the eye of visitors. Of course, she was also hoping to get Monsieur Courteline to taste her newest creations—a perfect balance of innovation and tradition. The year before, he had promised to serve as an ambassador for her bread in Paris, but things had never materialized.

As the two Parisians strolled along, observing the bustling preparations for the fair, they wondered why their host had so abruptly and inexplicably vanished. The last time Courteline had seen the mayor was during the fabulous dinner at Debasse's house. They had discussed their future business together over a *farandole* of delicacies. The profits could be staggering for both of them, and Debasse had been clear about his desire to move forward with this lucrative arrangement.

But where on earth had the mayor gone? Courteline wondered, looking around, peeved. Did he misconstrue Debasse's eagerness? He could not rid himself of the nagging thought that something had gone awry. Debasse had not been seen for days; it made no sense. This event was his moment to shine and he had vanished without a trace. Some surmised that Constance had fallen very ill and Debasse had been sitting by her bedside day and night, trying to alleviate his wife's excruciating pain.

But another gnawing doubt suddenly crept into Courteline's mind: was Debasse getting cold feet?

CHAPTER TWENTY-SEVEN

Debasse woke abruptly with a gasp, sweat beading down his neck. Clutching his down pillow, he caught his breath and craned his neck up from his horizontal position. He was comforted by the familiar surroundings: the crystal glass and carafe next to the brass lamp on the night table, his mahogany dresser, and the marble gilded empire clock chiming on the imposing chimney mantle.

The night had been awful; his dreams haunted by dark and menacing visions he could not dispel. A black hand had been chasing him, threatening to grab him and choke him as he ran through a maze that kept collapsing. He kept running, tripping, and hitting his head so hard; though it was a dream, his head still hurt this morning.

Rolling his head from side to side in pain, he wondered what was happening to him. He cautiously lifted his nightshirt and let out a discouraged huff. Constance was quietly resting in a winged *bergère* by his side, for she had spent the night taking care of him. She was surely tired but her forehead, pale and serene, framed by her dark brown hair and elegant eyebrows, gave the impression that she had been holding back.

He sat up a little, staring at her with his worried, furrowed brow. Although his body was anchoring him deep amid the numerous pillows, his mind was in turmoil, and he could not stop imploring Constance. Did she not realize that tomorrow, Saturday, was the *Fête de la Truffe, the* big day that would crown his mandate? he begged.

No one knew better than she how he had worked for months to get to this point: eight months of planning, reaching out to participants and vendors, encouraging local notables to attend and support the event, and, of course, finding creative ways to use the municipal budget to make this day the success he had envisioned.

It was, no doubt, the steppingstone to winning the next elections. If he were unable to deliver the speech he had honed so painstakingly, it would kill him! But was there a way around this? Because after all, no one else could deliver his speech … he trailed off, hoping that she would fill in the blank.

But his wife remained quizzically silent. So, he continued. Of course, he was conscious that the closing of the path had not pleased everyone, but he was only now beginning to understand the possible ramifications, he pleaded, glimpsing sideways at his wife and appealing to her sympathy. He feared Madame Sardelois would use his absence to campaign against him. In fact, he *knew* that she would. Her reputation as a widow was impeccable and she would draw on Trouvert's support. This was hopeless, he was stuck inside and powerless.

He looked again to his inscrutable wife for reassurance. Villagers would see him and talk, they would not understand what was really going on… he finished with a scowl.

But what was really going on? Constance asked softly, pulling her armchair closer to her husband's bed. Debasse could sense that she was in one of those moods. She had been dedicated to him all these years, she began, but in more recent times his depraved ways were becoming irksome to her soul. If he recalled, on several occasions she had suggested, even insisted, that he go to confession, for she saw penance as the only path to making amends. With all the carousing and drinking, not to mention the decision to close the Pilgrims' Path, he had lost his way, along with his sense of tradition and community.

In fact, deep inside she was convinced that this skin condition was a sign from above to urge him toward reflection. She placed her faith in higher powers; she had no doubt that he would eventually recover and regain his moral compass. He just needed help! She concluded cheerfully with a reassuring smile. Well, she had summoned the only person able to absolve him and help him through this delicate situation. Debasse stared back at her blankly as she finished her pronouncement. What "person" did she mean?

There was a light knock, and Trouvert walked through the door. He smiled benevolently, bowing to Constance as she left the room to leave the two alone. Earlier that morning, when Trouvert had seen Constance appear at his doorstep, he had known right away that the gates of Heaven were opening. And like Samuel, he would not ignore the call of the Lord.

Approaching the bed, he could not help but notice the redness of Debasse's neck and face. Sensing he was being examined, the mayor instinctively pulled up the sheet to conceal the source of his embarrassment. With his many years of experience helping his parishioners, Trouvert had learned to observe the signs of a troubled soul. His patience was genuine and his compassion deep for those willing to open up the inner recesses of their heart. Laying his biretta to the side, he moved a chair closer to the bed; as the dark folds of his large cassock elegantly enveloped his seat, it seemed that he was resting on air. He crossed his hands, and calmly waited for Debasse. But the mayor remained mute. After a long silence, Trouvert broke the ice.

Obviously, the past few days had been trying, but he had come to offer his help, the priest began in a soft voice. If the mayor examined the conflict that was plaguing him, God would afford him the strength to overcome these ailments, Trouvert urged. The mayor listened intently, his eyes half-closed. After a long pause, he grudgingly resigned himself to some degree of honesty.

If the word got out about his skin condition, villagers would start drawing all kinds of irrational conclusions, Debasse said, admitting to the fear that was crippling him. He understood that there was just one "leap of faith" to make; he must see his skin affliction as a prodigious sign of St. Calin's damning disapproval. Yet, if he did *that*, his reputation and everything he had worked for would be tarnished, he lamented.

On the other hand, if he confessed, would not all his words be locked in the confidence of confession? he questioned, as if suddenly discovering an old alchemist's secret. The priest nodded kindly in assent. Debasse still held back, unsure. How could he counteract suspicion when his absence was so blatant? But wait! Debasse suddenly let out a gasp. Yes! He could, he exclaimed. He knew exactly who could ensure that everything still went according to his plan!

He sat up, re-energized by this epiphany—the prospect of finding a quick way out of this unjustly shameful situation. And what better person, he muttered, to help him than Trouvert, the most respected spiritual figure in the region? Debasse motioned swiftly to the desk: it was over there, the speech—the papers were in a folder. It was all typewritten on single pages, he said, sitting up in his bed, a ray of hope illuminating his face. Trouvert was the most competent to manage the unfortunate circumstances that threatened to cloud his status and topple his election campaign. Debasse finished his appeal to the priest with eagerness as he searched his placid face for reassurance.

Trouvert acquiesced in solemn silence, crossing his long bony fingers together and reflecting for a few minutes. Debasse stared at this man who held his future in his hands. Yet, he could not help but be irritated by the insufferable devotion he had read on the priest's face— the same one he regularly saw on Constance's face. This entire situation was grotesque, he thought, and it made his itching even worse.

Deliver the speech for Debasse? the priest repeated to himself, thinking out loud. But how could he perform his speech, like only the mayor could? The priest got up and reached for the papers on the mayor's desk. Of course, he would keep to the spirit of the text that Debasse was handing him, but the mayor had to understand that, as the spiritual guide of Calignac, Trouvert would use his own expressions and turns of phrases. Moreover, he had a moral obligation to the community that he had been leading for decades. The priest finished, quickly leafing through the pages of the speech.

Debasse paused, uncertain how to respond. He hoped he could depend on the priest; indeed, there was no other viable option. Trouvert pulled out his rosary and leaned towards the patient with a kind look.

Closing his eyes in acceptance, Debasse welcomed the inescapable blessing and heard the priest whisper in his ear:

A speech was well worth a confession, *non?*

CHAPTER TWENTY-EIGHT

As the sun broke through the clouds to bathe the village square with a sudden wave of white light, Calignac bubbled with energy. Palpable excitement could be felt at every street corner: the much-anticipated *Fête de la Truffe* had finally arrived. Warmly dressed, the *rabassiers*—the truffle sellers and experts—bustled about like ants orchestrated by one common non-verbal signal: to prepare their stalls for the grand opening. They displayed their truffles on fresh beds of straw to accentuate their striking natural darkness. Beyond the fences that had been drawn, gawkers tried to stay patient behind small linen ropes tied to keep them from entering the alleys before the appointed time.

Yes, truffles were in the air, many joked as they tried to breathe in a taste of the black gems' heady fragrance. If the morning was dedicated to the sale of local truffles from around the region, the late afternoon was sure to attract a lot more attention, as it culminated with the prestigious prize for the best truffle of the year.

As villagers rubbed their hands to keep warm, they could not help but speculate about this year's winner. Who would take home the blue ribbon? Their curiosity and animation were heightened by Debasse's conspicuous absence. A week of relentless rumors left many wondering if he would reappear in time for the inauguration speech, one of the hallmarks of these merry festivities.

The Parisians had risen early that morning eager to witness all the stages of this provincial activity. The *Fête de la Truffe* was the reason they had come—or so Turgot had thought, oblivious to Courteline's business dealings with the mayor. Wrapped in their winter wool coats, they strolled along, scanning the displays of mounds of truffles. Courteline led the way, pretending to lay an expert eye on the stalls in front of him.

Experienced buyers were after a good bargain, he lectured ostentatiously. Although cursory, Courteline's academic readings on the topic granted him a social ease that kept Turgot in a state of voluntary servility. The dandy inhaled deeply: matchless vapor… definite, thick pungency… unique depth. A pure *Tuber Melanosporum*, the quintessential *Quercy* black truffle! His friend really knew it all, Turgot thought, proud to be associated with such a connoisseur.

Across the square, Adèle and Mathilde wove their way into the growing number of buyers, visitors, and jovial locals. Adèle examined the stalls, evaluating this year's bounty. There was an ideal ratio of quality to price, which remained consistent to the fair pricing that everyone had come to expect. Gently taking her grand-daughter's hand, Adèle pointed at different specimens and gave detailed descriptions of the desirable traits of each truffle.

Consistency and density were key attributes. There were also other factors to take into consideration, she continued. If the *rabassiers* would let you touch them, gauging by hand was the real test, she explained, placing a small black truffle in the little girl's hand. It felt wet and rough. The peculiarly odd sensation made Mathilde smile. While the smell of rot was an unmistakable sign of maturity, no aroma signaled the opposite. This particular truffle, with no detectable fragrance, should have been left in the earth longer to mature. Adèle pointed at a larger truffle on display in the background. Size was always an uncertain predictor of quality, whereas fragrance was paramount. However, there did exist an exceptional and rare specimen that, found at most once in a lifetime, combined both attributes.

Mathilde nodded and listened, enthralled. For the first time, she was enjoying the depth of knowledge that her grandmother shared. In the past, she had felt that information was forced on her in a way that constrained her free spirit. But today, things were different. Gazing around, surrounded by the plethora of choices and speci-mens, she was grateful that Bonne-Maman's lens was giving her an insight into this invisible underground world.

Mathilde's *rêverie* was interrupted by Courteline's smarmy presence. He had made his way over in the hope of gaining information. Adèle barely acknowledged him and continued to walk briskly, conversing with her granddaughter. Courteline lagged behind, trying to strike up a conversation.

Adèle owned beautiful land, he finally managed to insert, hoping to ingratiate himself by underscoring what he thought she valued most, which for once was not a completely inaccurate perception.

Oui? she exclaimed curtly. Was this a question or a statement? The corner of her lower lip betrayed how nettled she was at his vapid flattery. Their brief exchange was cut short when, around the corner, she caught sight of a particular specimen; she paused for a moment, weighing her options.

Had this truffle been washed? she inquired cautiously. Washing the truffle revealed its beautiful darkness and unleashed its heavenly ribbons of scent. But, it also irrevocably removed its protective surface and hastened the aging process of the truffle. The *trufficulteur* made a tsking sound as a rebuttal, denying any foul play.

Sensing that her interest was keen, he promptly placed the specimen in her hand. Slowly, Adèle examined it from every angle. The interior probably had veins of the darkest chocolate, Adèle mused. Yes, she had to admit that it looked small but flawless. After a swift exchange, a few nods and clucks, they agreed on a price. She shook the seller's hand and carried on with the small white bag nestled at the bottom of her wicker basket.

The bustle of busy clients seemed undisturbed by the cold gusts of wind that occasionally tore through the white tents. After some time, everyone made their way towards a small stage where the annual prize was to be announced. Each year, the coveted blue velvet ribbon would be presented to the winner, but everyone knew that the ribbon was a mere material manifestation, and that the true accolade was bestowed by Nature itself to its elect.

The *Commisaires es qualité*, the truffle expert officials, had examined all the truffles entered since dawn, sorting them out into specific categories by shape, size, and aroma. Black and white signs indicated the various categories and criteria used by the judges, all in descending pecking order. Anything above a quarter-pound in weight was deemed exceptional, but quality was cardinal.

The crowd now huddled around the perimeter of the stage in loud chatter. Mathilde noticed Béatrice at the bottom of the short stairs. The dog was rarely without her master; she stroked her soft back, looking around for Finoud. To the left, Léonard chatted noisily with the *Bouchère*, who stood erect guarding the stage while anxiously peering into the distance. So far, everything was going according to plan.

Where on earth was Debasse?

CHAPTER TWENTY-NINE

Suddenly, the chatter subsided, and the crowd quivered. Trouvert appeared, his celebratory cassock swirling in the wind as he ascended the raised rectangular platform. This would be much easier than any of his Sunday sermons, he thought, scanning the audience. For a minute, he stood there and smiled at the confusion he read on his parishioners' faces. Then he reached out and rang the brass bell. Once all eyes rested on him, he stared at the sheets of paper on the podium. He toyed with them for a minute, then pushed them aside and launched into his speech.

Today it was his great honor to stand before them to inaugurate this year's truffle celebration and contest. Debasse was most unfortunately unable to attend due to a sudden indisposition, but there was no doubt that the mayor shared in spirit this precious moment with Calignac.

Today, Trouvert stood in front of them to remind everyone why they had gathered here. Truffles were rare and pure. In the long history of our village, no other luxury had ever come close to this wild, rich source of perfection, he continued. And today, they had come together to honor Nature's most miraculous earthen treats.

The large audience stirred and listened with intent. Despite his gaunt frame, Trouvert's voice rose and his presence seemed to expand beyond his physical self, filling the entire space of the square so that each stone echoed his words.

But there was more, the priest pursued with poise. He was standing before them to remind them of what they had ignored time and time again. He was the voice of Calignac's slumbering conscience, here to unveil what they all knew deep down. Had the signs not been clear enough? Had the bleeding waters spouting out of St. Calin's fountain not warned them? Was it not true that few in the community had paused for a second to take stock of the situation? Trouvert's voice bounced off the surrounding walls of the marketplace.

No, of course not, he rebuked, they had stubbornly carried on with their business without paying attention to the indelible wrinkle left for all to see, this irrefutable evidence that things had gone awry. How could villagers have abandoned their faith in Nature and St. Calin? Trouvert's voice filled with gentle scolding. He was not here to berate the villagers or bruise their souls; rather, he wanted to reassure them that redemption was possible if they made amends today. He feared that the bleeding wounds of their conscience would deepen—*unless,* by a supreme effort, Calignac awoke from its stupor to set out on the right path again. It was possible; there was still time. Today could mark a new beginning. Today, joined together in celebration of the truffle, this community could change its destiny. Today, villagers could at long last renew their faith in Mother Nature and the earth that lay beneath their feet. Today, they could acknowledge their debt towards this beloved soil they trod on mindlessly, day in and day out.

Locked in reverent silence, the crowd swelled softly. United in a single breath, it stirred for a moment before coming up for air, as if teetering on the edge of a cliff. Then, a wave of applause broke out, sweeping across the square and reaching all corners. Even skeptical onlookers, standing staunchly with their arms crossed in front of Brévin's, felt the ripples of warmth that now pervaded the space into a palpable sense of communion.

The crowd rumbled with excitement as the priest gave the floor to the most venerable judge who slowly made his way to the center of the stage leaning on his knotty cane. A kind smile illuminated his sun browned and wrinkled face as he looked around and reveled in the lively babbling tumult. He nodded with satisfaction as the commotion subsided in preparation for the results of the truffle contest.

Judges had been working backstage all day, engrossed

in the meticulous pre-selection process. This year had seen an unprecedented number of finalists: seven contenders had made it to the final round of the competition. The atmosphere was electric. At the back, villagers craned their necks and stood on tiptoe not wanting to miss a word. Despite their jaded pretenses, the Parisians too could not help but hold their breath in anticipation, excited to witness the moment that justified the discomfort of their journey and the crudeness of their surroundings.

Joined by Didier, last year's winner, Trouvert showed the remaining judges to their seats on stage. A drumroll sounded, and each finalist was ceremoniously called one at a time. The reading of their names, particularly Léonard's, caused a commotion among the spectators. But, there were also a few newcomers that turned heads and loosened tongues. Then came Monsieur Montaigne, the squat but solid corn farmer who came year after year all the way from Sarlat to take his chances. Last, but not least, was Finoud. Understandably, his presence stirred up quite a reaction because entering such a competition was most unlike him.

The seven contestants lined up to face the public, staring off as they awaited the judges' verdict. Each held with care a wicker basket that held the precious truffle they were presenting. Although they had already spent much of the morning evaluating and deliberating, the three judges renewed their close inspection, leaning over each truffle like benevolent fairies. Chins thrust downward, they meticulously examined each specimen's particularities and merits.

As the committee gravely exchanged assessments, the crowd heaved a sigh of tingled exhilaration. The first two entries received a smirk of disdain, while Montaigne's truffle detained them for what seemed like an eternity. With the fourth truffle, Léonard's, they let out a sigh of obvious contentment and spontaneous appreciation. If the fifth and the sixth ones left them unimpressed, the seventh one, Finoud's, garnered their undivided attention. Mathilde's body quivered and her chest trembled with elation as her gaze remained fastened on the stage.

The judges were now beginning their final deliberations. Their backs to the crowd, some quickly bobbed their heads while others waved their hands, stamped their feet with agitation, or grunted with disapproval. A few exclamations of outrage in *patois* reached the first rows of the audience, punctuating the deafening silence. Mathilde felt her breath suspend. Finally, they nodded to one another with a scowl and turned around to face the restless crowd.

One after the other, they walked slowly in a line, back to the far end of the stage. They paused again in front of each contestant to check one last time that they had not overlooked anything. The most esteemed judge leaned over to scribble the name of the winner and runner-up on a little piece of paper, which he handed promptly to

Trouvert. Mesmerized, the villagers stared at the seven candidates, the three judges, and the priest for a long time.

All eyes were riveted on the royal blue velvet ribbon fluttering in the cold wind.

CHAPTER THIRTY

A light gust of icy wind swept across the square, freezing these moments of silence into endless eddies. Huddled like a sparrow against the folds of Adèle's wool cape, Mathilde stared back and forth between Finoud and Léonard: the best and the worst, shoulder to shoulder. A smug smile on his chapped lips, the hunter looked down at his truffle, resting on a small linen cloth in its basket. She could not and would not forget his betrayal. She despised him with all her heart. How could such a despicable man be paired with anything remotely beautiful and pure? All Mathilde could see now was the smug look of spite that shone deep in the hunter's eye sockets. Sensing the little girl cringe, Adèle placed her warm hand on Mathilde's shoulder.

The little girl's shiver expanded and rippled over the silence of the square as the crowd, holding its breath, stared intently at Trouvert who stood center stage, his rosary swinging from his waist.

Léonard cocked his head to the side and looked around, barely able to contain his confidence, winking at his supporters in the crowd clustered around Brévin. He rolled his head to the other side as he heard his name resound, just as he expected. He smacked his lips. This time, fortune was smiling on him—he just knew it. His intense frown had relaxed into an air of bold complacency as he stepped forward to eagerly grab Trouvert's hand.

But then, his eyes froze at the sight of a green ribbon. What was happening? He shuddered. Wait! Was this a joke? he muttered in utter disbelief. He looked around, baffled and confused. The consolation prize?! he snarled. His legs quivered and he felt as dizzy as one of the hares he hit over the head with a swift blow. This was a mistake, he thought, shaking his head in denial.

The crowd had now morphed into an indistinguishable mass behind him, blurry, undulating, and pulsing in a disorienting way. Paralyzed, he let Trouvert pin the green ribbon on his chest. Then he was motioned off the stage. In a daze, he stumbled down the steps. He staggered through the crowd, intercepted by those who insisted on shaking his hand. He could hardly get his bearings until Brévin led him to a chair and handed him a small *eau de vie* to help him recover. As he regained his wits, his blood filled his cheeks. He looked around for

Debasse. The mayor was not even here to correct this massive injustice… After all he had done for him… His jutted jaw retracted with anger.

Trouvert waited a few minutes for the excitement to settle. Then, he held out his long arms and fingers into the air in a dramatic gesture and went on. This year's winner had entered the most remarkable truffle he had personally ever had the privilege to witness. This year's winner was no less than *Finoud*, he declared with a large smile that hardly concealed his genuine joy.

He searched the crowd and called Finoud who had stepped off to tend to Béatrice. Not seeing him emerge, the crowd started chanting his name. When he appeared from behind the church, the crowd gently nudged him forward. The old man smiled as he approached the stage, treading lightly. He ascended the steps, followed by Béatrice who refused to miss any of the action. The priest reached to pin the blue ribbon onto the winner's lapel, but Finoud stopped him.

He turned to Béatrice, his faithful companion. She was the real winner, and she deserved the honor, he explained to the priest with a cheerful smile. The crowd applauded loudly as Trouvert bowed down to attach the ribbon onto Béatrice's collar rather than Finoud's. There was not a single villager who did not value the labor and skill of dogs in identifying the location of truffles. The dog sat lowering her *truffe*, known by the French as the dog's nose. With dignity, she welcomed this reward as the remarkable distinction that it was. Thus adorned, she let out joyful barks as the other judges assembled around Finoud to congratulate him.

Then, extending both hands, the senior judge lifted the winning truffle out of the basket, high into the air, and walked along the edge of the stage for everyone to admire it. It was miraculous: larger than any they had seen in years, he declared. The crowd stirred like a moving sea, as everyone stood on tiptoe to gain a better view of the specimen. The truffle weighed just under 34 ounces; its firm texture was perfect and its fragrance the purest, the judge proclaimed.

Fixed on the wondrous object, Mathilde's eyes twinkled as she remembered the tiny round black truffles that she had once seen on the kitchen table at Easter before they disappeared, sliced into an *omelette*. They looked no larger than plump walnuts. This truffle, now resting in the judge's hands, looked like a large clump of raspberries, dark, shiny, and potent. Fighting a coughing fit, Adèle breathed in deeply, spurred on as she sensed Mathilde's shoulder blades ever so slightly contract and expand with excitement. Mathilde's eyes were riveted to the stage, oblivious to her grandmother's cough. After this triumphant walk, the judge put the truffle back down carefully, as if it were a delicate *Limoges* porcelain.

Staring down at his feet, Finoud ran his rough palm across his forehead. Taking a step forward, he thanked the committee and bowed graciously to the cheering audience. Before anyone could object, he wrapped up his treasure and swiftly walked off, his bundle close to his heart, leaving everyone in disbelief. Just like that, he was gone and, along with him, any chance to get another peep at such a perfect specimen.

He preferred moonlit solitude to the tumult of popular acclaim.

CHAPTER THIRTY-ONE

Over the next few days, the villagers' minds were consumed with feverish excitement over the *Fête de la Truffe*'s unexpected outcome. It seemed like a dream. Animated debates sprang up at Brévin's, who had opened his doors much earlier in light of the unexpected circumstances. Everyone speculated over Finoud's miraculous specimen, much to the delight of the two curious Parisians who had started making daily appearances. Bored and welcoming titillating gossip, the two soaked up the local scene.

The extraordinary characteristics of Finoud's truffle had everyone spell-bound, for no one else had seen such a prodigy of Nature. Yes, it had been a long time, the elders agreed, nodding as they reminisced about the past and compared this year with the previous years' fairs. But what confounded everyone was the fact that Finoud owned no land. Where could he possibly have found such a treasure? That was the question burning on everyone's lips. Could he have stolen it?

Non, non, the elders countered with wisdom, shaking their heads curtly. Finoud was not that kind, and never had been. His reputation was as good as gold. He had to have found it on communal ground, they concluded decisively. If Finoud's find was shrouded in mystery, one thing was clear: all villagers without exception would have given an arm and a leg to know the exact location of his discovery. The field it came from could potentially yield more bounty, and that information was worth its weight in gold.

This heated atmosphere was compounded by the fact that Debasse's condition remained a mystery. As a result, the village stood effectively without any governance. Since Trouvert had mentioned the mayor's absence yesterday, there had been no additional light shed on his state of health, so many now assumed that he must be seriously ill.

Despite numerous attempts, no one, including his good friend Didier, had been able to pry any information from Montrelazet. The *Docteur's* lips remained sealed. As sole source of official information, Montrelazet had instead skillfully redirected the conversation towards the celebration of St. Calin and the upcoming evening at Bonne-Maman's that Thursday night.

While the general mood of the villagers was effervescent with curiosity, Léonard sat at the bar, wallowing in self-pity and seething with rage.

Brévin genuinely sympathized with Léonard's bewilderment. How could Finoud possibly have found such a truffle not only perfect in texture, but also exceptional in fragrance? The café owner leaned over to hand him another espresso. The hunter had trouble keeping his emotions in check as his unexpected loss was not the only thing that left a bitter taste in his mouth. Most *rabassiers* struggled a lifetime to harvest decent truffles and Finoud, a simple man, a shepherd who walked the fields, leading his flock of sheep, had managed to pull off the unthinkable!

All the talk of truffle hunting revived Courteline's fantasy of unearthing a real truffle himself. Maybe there was still time before leaving this Godforsaken province? he thought, eying Léonard from the side. This rough and uncivilized man, this beast of the woods, could be a valuable source of information. There was a lull in the conversation when the postman came through the door. The post office had received an urgent telegram for Courteline.

A telegram had arrived? For him? From whom? the Parisian exclaimed with self-importance as he rose to his feet and wrapped his heavy silk scarf around his wide neck.

He walked out, savoring the thought that his abrupt and dramatic exit created suspense in a village where things were markedly less simple than they had initially appeared.

CHAPTER THIRTY-TWO

High in the house on a limestone hill, the front bell rang, which was unusual, given that many simply knocked. Mathilde rushed to the door. Seeing no one, she stepped outside for a minute and looked around. Finally, she noticed to the side a neatly wrapped package; someone had nestled it against the wall, lest it rain. Finoud often left fresh eggs for them, but this package looked altogether different. She cautiously picked it up and brought it into the kitchen where Adèle and Bernadine were reorganizing the pantry. Adèle climbed down from her step stool and approached the table where the little girl had placed the peculiar bundle, equally intrigued. Mathilde could sense her surprise.

Carefully, Adèle started untying the linen wrapping but immediately stopped short, struck by the distinct smell emanating from it. She lifted the package and slowly brought it to her expert nose. Then, she handed it to Bernadine, who raised her eyebrows. Mathilde craned her neck with impatience; she too wanted to understand what was unraveling before her eyes. Adèle delicately removed the last of the wrapping, revealing what looked like an extraordinarily shiny black gem. Mathilde was mesmerized by this unexpected sight. Suddenly something clicked.

This truffle bore a strange resemblance to Finoud's! Mathilde exclaimed. But why leave such a precious item unattended at their front door? she pursued pressing her grandmother for answers. Adèle observed Mathilde as the little girl struggled to connect the dots. This one had been theirs all along, she said with an enigmatic smile. Adèle got up and disappeared into the pantry for a few minutes.

Mathilde's eyes could not stop marveling at the deep black color of the prize truffle. She reached out to touch the grainy, rubbery surface of the truffle, rubbing it against her soft fingertips. When Adèle came back, she held in her hand a small pebble-like stone that she placed in Mathilde's palm. It was time to visit Finoud, she added softly. He would teach her everything there was to know, she promised.

Down in the village, Courteline headed hastily to the post office. Who was sending him a cable? Few people knew that he was spending time in this remote region, and he intended to keep it that way. Besides getting the supply of fresh produce for his Parisian restaurants, he planned on taking full credit for any gastronomic delicacies and recipes he stole from Calignac. He tore open the yellow envelope that the postman handed him. There was only a single line of bold typed characters. His vision became blurry, and his blood froze. What?!

A few minutes later Courteline rang Debasse's bell imperiously; when Constance opened the door, he pushed his way past her. She scrambled after him, trying to bar the staircase. But Courteline neither cared nor listened to her injunctions. Courteline climbed up the stairs, pushed the French doors open, and found the mayor standing at his desk, organizing piles of correspondence and paperwork.

After days of confinement, Debasse looked up, welcoming the Parisian's visit—at least, until the otherwise well-mannered Courteline unleashed his rage without preamble. He had come at once—the situation was beyond catastrophic, Courteline yelled. He, the greatest Parisian gourmet, was now at risk of losing his reputation that had taken years to build. He could not stand by and do nothing, he ranted with indignation.

Two of his customers had fallen violently ill after eating the game from Calignac. To be more precise: their bodies had been covered with a mysterious red rash for the past week.

CHAPTER THIRTY-THREE

Debasse stared at the Parisian, stunned. What, a rash? Did it resemble anything like this? He motioned to his bare forearm as he rolled up the long sleeve that came down over his knuckles. Courteline recoiled with panic. What? Debasse had it too? At least, this explained the mayor's absence from the village during the *Fête de la Truffe*.

While Courteline wallowed in disgust, Debasse followed his own train of thought. It was at that moment that something clicked in his mind. So it was the game that had made him sick and given him such an embarrassing rash. And since he had been the only one to fall ill, it had to have been the pheasant he had indulged. He remembered how the Parisian had declined it that fateful night during their exclusive gathering; pheasant had never been his cup of tea. The other guests had followed his example, satiated and unable to accommodate the seventh course of such a sumptuous and extravagant dinner.

For a long time, Debasse had thought, like the *Docteur*, that his condition might be a vicious virus. But this now looked more like… food poisoning. As this realization slowly sunk in, he frowned in disbelief. How could one get food poisoning from fresh game? Constance had warned him from the very start, hadn't she? His corporeal affliction mirrored the corruption of his mind, a mind that had taken the wrong path by going against the values of Calignac, she had insisted in her gentle yet unyielding voice. Given that the *Docteur*'s treatment had hardly made a difference, he had wondered if she was not right after all.

Now though, with these three documented cases of food poisoning attributed to three separate animals, the whole picture was beginning to shift. Was the food poisoning an indication of some more mysterious force at work? A strange mixture of solace and paranoia washed over him—solace that his soul was redeemable after all, but fear that there was clearly some outside force at work actively trying to derail his plans.

Meanwhile, Courteline had helped himself to a few glasses of walnut *eau de vie* to calm his nerves. He kept rubbing his hands and face with his lacy handkerchief as if to ward off any contagion. This situation was absolutely untenable, Courteline declared with scorn. All this drama with the fountain, then Debasse's inexplicable desertion, and now this predicament that jeopardized his life's work and his reputation among the Parisian *élite*! Really, this was the last straw—their deal was *off*, and he did not care one bit what happened after that, Courteline lashed out, incensed.

Wiping beads of sweat from his glowing forehead with his sleeve, Debasse felt the blood drain from his face as his heart pounded rapidly. He had to nip Courteline's fears and doubts in the bud. He looked straight into Courteline's eyes with the authority and charisma that he could still summon despite his extreme fatigue.

It had really been just one bad batch, he began, trying to downplay the consequences of the situation. He regretted this deplorable incident but all other supplies had been beyond reproach. Was it not true that for the last year, he had supplied goods of the most impeccable quality to Courteline, week after week?

Of course, it was most unfortunate that these two customers should be affected by similar symptoms. All in all, the real cause of this preposterous skin condition was debatable, and there was no concrete evidence that connected Courteline's customers' rashes to Calignac game. Debasse knew that Courteline knew the truth, and maybe Courteline's chef knew it too, but he was not about to let a couple of cases of food poisoning ruin this arrangement.

There was simply no proof, Debasse continued, and it would *never* happen again. He had already put in place new even more stringent measures to control quality, he said. In a few years, they both would laugh at this miserable and insignificant episode. Frankly, they could not just stop the whole adventure at the first hint of difficulty. Throwing away their painstaking endeavors would be pure folly! Debasse sensed a calmness washing over himself as he listened to his own logic.

As for the rash, there was a remedy, Debasse continued, reaching for a small bottle of medication that the *Docteur* had left him. Courteline waved him back in disgust. Courteline had to believe him, Debasse urged. This was the miracle drug, a time-worn recipe, a potion made from wild herbs found in the woods and boiled in the holy water from the village fountain. He finally caught Courteline's attention. The rash was almost entirely gone, Debasse pointed out, showing his arm as evidence of his recovery. Adèle had reminded the *Docteur* about the existence of this recipe from an old manuscript St. Calin had written.

Courteline stared at Debasse. Adèle? Again? What irony! To think that the mayor of Calignac owed his salvation to that little woman? Courteline was dubious.

Debasse stared back, as if struck by lightning. Yes, Adèle again. He had never thought of it that way, but now the coincidence seemed to hit him deep in his stomach.

Well, *he*, Courteline, had absolutely no intention of gambling away his reputation, he smirked contemptuously as he headed towards the door. He needed bullet-proof guarantees. He could not bear another minute of this nonsense—the mysteries of St. Calin were everywhere: the fountain with bloody waters, and now this absurd rash. He wanted to leave as soon as possible but since the trains were not running every day, he would have to wait until the weekend, until Saturday, to leave this place of utter nonsense. Everything in this village was backwards, Courteline snapped.

Sensing that it could very well be the end, Debasse fell on his knees. He would find a solution, he would give him guarantees, he pleaded, if only Courteline would grant him a few days, five days… But the Parisian turned his back on him and soon his steps grew fainter down the hallway. The mayor slowly rose to his feet and stared out the window at the tall and majestic cedar tree that towered over the estate's magnificent grounds. He had a sinking feeling.

He had to get to the bottom of this without further delay.

CHAPTER THIRTY-FOUR

Léonard had dropped him off at the gate. From the road, Debasse caught sight of Adèle and Mathilde standing outside near the woodpiles. It was the first time he had been out in over two weeks, and it had taken a lot to convince Constance that he was fully recovered from the rash and without long-term effects. Now that his stamina had returned, he could not bear to stay inside a minute longer.

He avoided looking at himself in the mirror because he shuddered at how the recent affliction could well have disfigured him. Most of all, he was preoccupied with Courteline's threats to call off their deal. But what especially nagged him was the Parisian's belief that someone had deliberately sabotaged their venture; Courteline had mentioned a division among the people, and complained that loyalty to the mayor seemed to be waning. Courteline was also troubled by a coincidence: what were the odds that Adèle could magically produce the perfect cure at the height of the mayor's vulnerability? A little too convenient, would you not say?

The thought that someone had gone out of their way to thwart his enterprise had never crossed his mind, but now, it seemed like a real possibility. Admittedly, many villagers did not agree with the decisions that he had forced through the municipal council. Also, he knew from his wife's passionate recounting of Trouvert's galvanizing and eloquent speech at the *Fête de la Truffe* that his presence during the festivities had not been missed as much as he had hoped. After a restless night, having thought long and hard about it, his instincts told him that, if a solution were to be found, it would be through Adèle's involvement. This time, he would try to be more honest. At this stage, he had nothing to lose. He clutched his gold pocket watch; it had always brought him good luck.

Right after breakfast with Mathilde, Adèle had gone out to the large woodpile. Chopping wood kept her alert. But recently, she favored the maul over the ax, which she found too dangerous, as Gérard whetted the blade regularly. Regardless, she was pleased to have Mathilde join her. With authority, she placed the maul in the little girl's hands and stepped back. Few understood that using the tool was not so much about strength but rather about balance and precision. As Mathilde swung the sledgehammer, Adèle watched the log split along an even fracture line. Yes, this little girl had it in her blood, she mused, marveling at the cadence and timing of her swing.

As Debasse pushed open the old wrought iron gate and headed for the side of the house, Adèle paused and turned to him. Surprised to see the mayor after such a long absence, she wondered what he could possibly want. As he came closer, she naturally walked forward to greet him. Yes, it was good to see him looking so healthy—but after just a week into his recovery, was it prudent to venture outside?

He had come to express his gratitude for her thoughtfulness in reminding Montrelazet of St. Calin's old book of remedies. The potion had done wonders; he extended his unblemished hands as proof of his regained health. Suspecting that the mayor had come for something specific, Adèle turned to Mathilde and instructed her to take some wood inside.

He had a business opportunity, Debasse began, clearing his throat, and raising his head to meet Adèle's gaze. It was, in fact, a golden one, he added quickly, with the practiced warmth Adèle knew so well from his campaign speeches.

When he had met Courteline a few years back, they had decided to share the exceptional quality and excellence of the region's *terroir* with Parisians. The goal, he said, was for Calignac to come out of its status of relative obscurity. No longer a blip on the map of France, it would stand out, receiving credit for its exceptional resources and achieving the visibility it deserved.

Debasse continued making his case. Could she imagine, he pursued with confidence, that at this very moment, Paris was already discovering the greatness of *Quercy?* Not to mention that the proceeds could be high, very high in fact, he added.

Adèle owned one of the richest plots of land in the area and she could help furnish the supply of game and mushrooms. Her compensation would be considerable. Indeed, how else could she take care of such an old house in need of constant maintenance, he asked, pointing to the roof. Winter had not been kind to the mortar and would have to be repointed, he remarked, eyeing the dormers. And then there was also Mathilde's future to consider…

Yes, she couldn't agree more. The old walls that she had fought to preserve all these years were no trifling matter and, of course, Mathilde's education had recently been on her mind, she responded in a grave voice. Debasse lit up, energized as he listened hopefully to words that sounded full of promise. Would he care to tell her more about what he had in mind? she prompted with curiosity. Of course, today, he absolutely needed to be forthright with her.

Well, *she* had certainly been very transparent with him all these years, she smiled candidly. So why beat around the bush? Before Debasse could add anything, Adèle went on, not pausing for a breath. Why not share his grand scheme with her? Was she correct in assuming that seeking out fresh game was only the tip of the iceberg, so to speak? She knew he had bigger plans, on a far grander scale. The rash outbreak raging in Paris was evidence of that, she went on, with a smile playing at the corners of her delicate lips.

Debasse's jaw dropped; his eyelids seemed to twitch for a second. Whatever did she mean? How on earth did she know about the rash outbreak in Paris? Without seeking an answer, she pressed on with a sense of urgency.

Oh, but how very clever! she exclaimed with feigned admiration. Right from the start, he had seen well beyond the paltry amount that Courteline had come to offer him. Of course, he had agreed to make a few personal sacrifices, especially at the critical time of the *Fête de la Truffe*, voluntarily subjecting himself to affliction by a skin rash—after all, he had to ensure that the potion would work wonders, had he not? Soon the quest for game would recede into the background because, as he had realized, its selling potential paled in comparison to that of the potion. This miracle cure for such afflictions would make him a very rich man indeed.

Debasse's shoulders slumped as Adèle's words disarmed him. What was this all about? His vision blurred, unable to comprehend the machinations that she was so readily attributing to him. All he could focus on was that she had not yet rejected his proposal. Was he dreaming or going mad?

Adèle nodded and smiled. Yes, he did look a little tired, ailments aside, she confided, as she invited him to walk back to the gate. The people of Calignac did not realize how lucky they were to have such a devoted mayor. In fact, she was quite certain that everyone needed to be reminded of the depth of his personal sacrifice and commitment. She would be sure to share the details of his *larger* plan at the *Soirée des petits fours*—unless, of course, he preferred to keep everything between them.

Honestly, he could not remember the rest of the conversation. He found himself entering Calignac, completely stunned. He walked slowly as his mind tried to process his encounter with Adèle. What on earth had she meant? Gradually, his features tightened: the scope of Adèle's insinuations, the gravity, her roundabout allusions to his poaching and trading with Courteline, and now this potion deal she had conjured out of nowhere…

Then it finally dawned on him: she was essentially accusing him of scheming to exploit this ancestral recipe for profit. It was as if she had rewritten his story, ascribing intentions where he had had none. If she spread these rumors, he would be held publicly accountable for his underhanded and unscrupulous greed, for his plunder of the region's natural and historical wealth. If the electorate got a hold of this information, he was doomed. He tried to repress the wave of panic that was coming over him.

It all became clear: he would be exposed as a fraud; his whole political reputation as the man of the people would go up in smoke!

CHAPTER THIRTY-FIVE

The following morning, Mathilde sat in the corridor, her eyes riveted on the clock as the minutes ticked away. She held tightly onto the little box in which her grandmother had placed the enigmatic pebble. At the strike of nine o'clock, she would leave as Bonne-Maman had instructed, to meet Finoud out in his shed. As she leapt outside, Mathilde skipped across the field, her lungs filled with the frosty air. Soon she caught sight of Finoud's shed. She knocked a few times and then gently pushed open the old plank door to find him threading sheep's wool.

From the back, his figure looked so youthful, and she waited until he paused and turned around. She reached into the tiny box and eagerly handed what Bonne-Maman had given her without explanation. He smiled and let his fingers play with it pensively for a few moments. So, what did she want to know? he asked with a mischievous grin. Everything! she responded with spirited innocence.

Taking her by the arm, he showed her to a small stool. After giving her a ball of raw wool, he watched her shape the thread by twisting and pulling as he had taught her. As she kept her hands busy, Finoud sat back on a wicker chair nearby.

Truffles were a little like the rest, he began. What did he mean? she asked. Time, he continued. Could, for example, the sheep's wool collected this morning suddenly transform into the neat ball of yarn that Bernadine knitted in front of the fire? No, it was a slow, painstaking process like much else of value. Mathilde became pensive.

Time was needed to make buds germinate, to burnish the patina of any wood, not to mention truffles. Did she remember what they had talked about in the past? Regarding trees? Finoud asked, pointing through the shed's window to the dark and elegant walnut tree. This tree stood there naked, stripped of its leaves and fruit by winter, Finoud noted. But there was no mistaking that under the darkened bark, time was working its magic, adding layers, discarding any superfluous material. The sap would soon flow out and burst through its veins with the arrival of spring. There was no mistaking this desolate appearance—the tree was only dormant.

Similarly, Mathilde's mind was growing in unexpected ways, branching out and developing new ways of thinking. She had started to become more resilient and apt at untangling intricate situations. Mind and tree grew organically, constantly redefining themselves with respect to their environment and circumstances. The tall walnut tree blown by the north wind tilted so as not to break. Likewise, Mathilde's mind gained perspective and flexibility when tested, he continued. She had managed to let go of the pain of losing Clémentine and felt a deeper connection to the wooded vale: a feeling of belonging to the earth. Painful processes required cheerful forbearance, he added with fondness.

But Nature relinquished her secrets only to careful observers, expecting that they would use them wisely—neither out of pride nor vanity. Before thinking about unearthing a truffle, one had to fully understand the earth, its rhythms and movements, its withholdings and its spontaneous gifts. Born out of Nature's whimsical genius, an exceptional truffle required loving patience as it emerged from the soil to the surface. But how could one pinpoint the location of a truffle? Mathilde asked, looking directly at Finoud. They were not visible to the naked eye.

It was just that she did not know how and where to look, Finoud responded with a smile.

CHAPTER THIRTY-SIX

A good eye required training, Finoud continued gently. Most people expected to notice subtleties without looking hard for the clues that Nature generously left behind as a road map for the conscientious observer. But Nature was disinterested; it did not intend for mankind to extrapolate any hidden meaning or to manipulate its bounty for personal gain. With every large or small miracle revealed, Nature remained unconcerned by man's petty ambitions. Happy were the men who caught sight of this magic and could glimpse the beauty, strength, and economy of its harmonious workings.

Did Mathilde know that, for instance, when the ground under an oak tree appeared barren, it was ironically *more* likely to bear in its bosom an exceptionally rare treasure? Finoud winked, prodding the little girl's memory. She frowned, puzzled, but after a few seconds, her face brightened as she made the connection. Finoud was alluding to the dried-up oak trees that grew in Bonne-Maman's wooded vale, which, like the village elders who hunched over as they walked, bore all the weight of years of unexpected hardship and windy storms.

Finoud continued aloud, as if reading her thoughts: when all has passed, when death has washed away man's presumptuous attempts to leave his mark on the earth, these trees would still be there, standing under the constellations of stars that lit the wooded vale on a clear night.

A man from the outside—a Parisian, for instance—would surely fail when looking at this prosperous earth, because his cosmopolitan eyes, avid but blind, focused on the apparent sterility of the ground encircling the oak trees. But if truffles seem to thrive in dry earth, Mathilde knew well that not all dry spots necessarily produced tons of truffles, Finoud reminded her.

Truffles were rare; they required a particular convergence of special natural factors: the quality of the earth, its density and moistness, the oak tree roots on which the subterranean mushroom affixed itself, and then the cumulative and recent humidity levels of that year. The truffle Finoud had presented at the fair was a perfect specimen and had benefited from these felicitous circumstances. Too little rain condemned truffles to remain small and underdeveloped, while too much moisture caused them to rot and shrivel, he explained. What a fragile balance… Mathilde sighed, remembering the conversation between Courteline and Bonne-Maman.

So, if one could not grow truffles, how could one discover them? Mathilde whispered.

Finoud glanced down at his rugged hands bearing many deep cracks. Some searchers waited for the appearance of the famous blue flies that alighted precisely where truffles grew, while others sought the help of a pig or dog that could smell them beneath the ground and dig them up. Some were convinced that truffles would grow back in the same location year after year, so they left wheat seeds behind to mark the spot. The seeds would then germinate, reminding the truffle hunter of the exact location.

Aha, so that was it! Mathilde thought, in a moment of enlightenment. She recounted to Finoud how she had caught Léonard in the wooded vale tossing some mysterious "golden dust" over his shoulder. Not only had he murdered her beloved fox, but she had clearly seen him mark a truffle location on their land with seeds, she explained with controlled anger.

Finoud paused his work for a second and gazed intently at Mathilde. Adèle had sent her to him precisely to further her education, he went on. But she had to remember that what was special was not finding truffles, but rather coming to love the journey of the soul as it discovered the numerous, ingenious, and careful ways in which Nature wrapped up her presents for mankind. Finoud gently grabbed the small pebble-like stone that had piqued Mathilde's curiosity and placed it in her hand. Yes, it was a truffle. And what she did next would decide the fate of the wooded vale. Truth and beauty—so fragile—would require the protective cover of lies. Finoud gazed at her intensely. Now, it was just a question of finding the right trap to snare their target. They needed to find the right foe whose vanity and indiscretion would inadvertently ensure that the secret of the vale remain sealed forever.

Of course, it would look like pure coincidence, he chuckled as Mathilde's eyes sparkled in the afternoon light.

CHAPTER THIRTY-SEVEN

Standing at the window, Adèle watched the evening fog settle in and the shepherd's star rise bright and lucid. It was the eve of St. Calin's day. She looked at the clock and glided by the gleaming wooden staircase, smelling the many coats of warm wax that Bernadine had applied over the preceding days with an eye to the celebration. Hanging majestically, the large tapestries that led the way to the kitchen had been dusted. Adèle could hear the cheerful voices of Bernadine, Madame Sardelois, Mathilde, and Bruno as they stood gathered around the table watching Gérard pour Didier's new wine into large earthen pitchers.

Under the imposing chandelier that illuminated the entrance hall, Adèle welcomed the guests that bustled through the heavy front door into the dining room, where Bernadine had lit a huge blazing fire in the stately stone fireplace. The *Boulangère* rubbed her hands vigorously while Trouvert removed his woolen coat. Wasn't the smell of pine needles crackling in the fire invigorating? she commented on the relaxing fragrance that was filling the room. Indeed, winter was taking a turn for the worse, and this might very well be the coldest St. Calin's day in the history of Calignac, he responded, nodding in assent.

Bernadine and Adèle joined them, eager to spend a few relaxing minutes before everyone else arrived. While Bernadine and the *Boulangère* merrily caught up on news, Adèle was only too happy to see her old friend Trouvert. Yes, another year had passed and here they were, yet again around the same fire to celebrate the village Saint. He smiled back at her pensive observation. This year's celebration would be remarkable in many ways, Adèle continued, as if responding to Trouvert's thoughts. She then led her dear friend to the table laden with *petits fours*. The room was now quickly filling up and lively conversation began to percolate.

Their *tête à tête* was interrupted by the boisterous arrival of the *Bouchère*, followed by several other villagers. The *Bouchère* marched in, eager to claim recognition for organizing the *Fête de la Truffe* that year. She looked around for Debasse, but to no avail. No mayor, no laudatory speech, she thought in a huff. Irritated, she wondered who would pay her the credit she deserved as she scanned the crowd for the brown velvet jacket that Debasse wore on such occasions. There were other people missing too: namely, Léonard and Finoud. When would Finoud reveal the origin of the fabulous truffle that had received first prize? the *Bouchère* prattled suspiciously to her small circle. It was stolen, stolen, she ranted. Nothing new under the sun, the *Boulangère* thought, shrugging her shoulders dismissively. A few steps away, a *petit four* in each of his plump hands, the *Pharmacien* enjoyed a lively conversation with the *Docteur* and Turgot as the Parisian displayed his knowledge of the vestiges of Roman ruins in the region.

Courteline and Debasse, with the lovely Constance on his arm, suddenly appeared in the room. Yet they hardly seemed to acknowledge each other. After a week left to his own devices, Courteline was still seething from his previous meeting with Debasse, when the mayor had begged and pleaded for more time. But now Debasse had turned yet again inexplicably silent. Courteline grumbled under his breath, irritated at this sudden and incomprehensible shift. He, the great gourmet, was being ignored and shunted to the side like a mere peon, he thought.

Revealing nothing of his contempt, he quickly glided to the side, drawn in by the wafting aroma of warm delicious bread loaves. Debasse forced a smile as he walked further into the room, stopping to greet the villagers, who were relieved to see him up and about. He seemed to have his stamina back, they whispered as they scanned him for clues.

From across the room, Montrelazet observed his patient with a sense of satisfaction. Although the cause of Debasse's rash remained a mystery, he was pleased to see that Constance's complexion seemed healthier than ever.

Leaving her husband surrounded by villagers, Constance headed towards Trouvert. She was eager to find out the latest details about St. Calin's procession that would take place the following day.

She was in for the surprise of her life.

CHAPTER THIRTY-EIGHT

Seeing all eyes rest on him, Debasse stood up and straightened his shoulders. The rash was completely gone, and no one knew about it, he tried to reason with himself. Although… He could not spot Adèle in the room, but after a short time, he felt the burning intensity of her gaze resting between his shoulder blades. Coming back to Adèle's house reminded him of their painful exchange the day before regarding his personal business proposition: he admitted to the desire to secure her wooded vale for his personal venture, but the potion? The outcome of the conversation had been rather disastrous, he had to admit, nothing like he had planned. His re-election hinged on his ability to negotiate the curveballs that fate had so inexplicably thrown at him, yet again. And it *had* been fate—a rather obstinate fate to say the least—an accumulation of relentless obstacles that had risen up mysteriously as if to frustrate his ambitions.

He continued to shake hands mechanically, realizing that he could not be detoured by such introspective questions, moving on to the *Boulanger*. Was he still thinking of exporting his bread up to Paris? He could help with the logistics, he offered, feigning generosity. Any false promises to guarantee his advancement, he thought. Just then, the *Boulangère*, his wife, approached to inquire about his health. Yes, he had to admit that the numerous initiatives he had undertaken for Calignac had been all-consuming. She nodded with eager approval. He smiled back, grateful to find a sympathetic ear.

On the other side of the room next to the bread table, Courteline stood erect, flamboyantly swank in his three-piece suit. He bitterly resented being trapped in Calignac and felt that this stupid, inane little civilization had personally plotted against him. Seeing Bernadine nearby, he latched onto Adèle's excellent cook in a final attempt to extract from her whatever secrets she might be willing to part with. After courteously indulging him for a few minutes, Bernadine rubbed her hands on her long apron, turned her back to him, and returned to the kitchen. She came back out again, her arms laden with large enticing platters, delicious fragrances wafting in her wake. The children lent a hand passing them around so everyone could taste the unique flavors of each variety of Bernadine's *petits fours*. A few villagers huddled together near the fire in good company, appreciating the service, while others moved around constantly, like butterflies feeding on many different flowers.

Although he was certainly not the grateful kind, Courteline was glad that his palate was piqued by the deep, dark, full-bodied Cahors wine. If the thought of being poisoned crossed his mind for a few seconds, he laughed it off and resolved that indulging in sensual pleasures would be therapeutic. Leaning into the wall, he now closed his eyes and swallowed one of Bernadine's *petits fours*, hoping to identify her secret ingredients. Intellectually, he understood Bernadine's concept for this feast: a single motif explored in an array of variations. That night, everything was made with puff pastry: the snails, herbs, truffles, and mushrooms. Everyone savored mouthfuls and nosefuls of the enchantingly fragrant portions floating around the room.

Suddenly, Adèle stepped to the front of the room and asked for a moment of silence. She paused briefly as wine was passed around in elongated glasses, allowing the crowd to settle. She was delighted to have them in her home for this evening of celebration and thanked them for their presence. What better time to celebrate our patron St. Calin! she exclaimed with warmth and energy, looking around at the villagers with *petits fours* in hand. Bernadine's *cuisine* was there to delight their taste buds and remind them of the many blessings bestowed on Calignac, she went on with solemnity.

Indeed, thanks to the generous help of many contributors, Calignac continued to thrive; the *Fête de la Truffe* had attracted quite a few connoisseurs, drawn by their spirit of tradition and the village's love of nature. If this year's fair had not attracted as many as in the past, Adèle noted, this was no doubt a temporary setback. Indeed, Calignac's most hardworking and selfless mayor was one hundred percent committed to the demands of such an exceptional community, she continued. Seeing the numbers of the *Fête de la Truffe* decline, the mayor's response had been quick and his resolve fierce, she complimented eloquently. He has done it again, Adèle finished, extending her hand towards the mayor to give him the floor.

The mayor had some very exciting news for them tonight, she hinted. During Adèle's toast, an odd, yet familiar feeling rushed through his veins as he perceived the thrust of what she implied. For a brief moment, he gazed back at her in disbelief but quickly regained his composure. His large hands ran down his suit to smooth out the fabric creases over his prodigious belly. He passed his hand elegantly over his forehead. The beads of sweat were hardly noticeable to anyone but herself, Adèle thought.

Debasse cleared his throat and his eyes focused under his large bushy brows. As his mind raced ahead, he desperately hoped for a way out of the situation, but he knew he had his back up against the wall. There really was no alternative, was there? he thought, his heart throbbing as he started to speak.

Mechanically, he thanked Adèle and Bernardine for hosting such a wonderful feast.

He thanked the outstanding contributors to the *Fête de la Truffe*, who year after year generously gave their support to such a deep-rooted tradition. Very much like Calignac's community, the *Fête de la Truffe* could not be neglected, he continued, as if inspired.

He could not believe that Adèle had managed to put words in his mouth, but it was actually happening, he thought furiously. At this moment, he understood even more clearly than before that he was at a crossroads: either he re-opened the paths, or he would have to sacrifice the possibility of his re-election. There was no point in resisting. So as if it had been the most natural thing in the world, he shared with the villagers his plans to reopen the ancestral Pilgrims' Path. There was no doubt, it was in Calignac's best economic and cultural interests.

Debasse's complete turnaround was a shock and for a few minutes, villagers stared at each other speechless. But before they could do anything, Adèle stood up and walked over to Debasse to wring his hands with great emotion. After many months at odds, they stood together, seemingly reconciled. After a moment of hesitation, everyone broke into applause. What a beautiful moment of unity this all was!

Standing to the side, sipping his drink, Courteline watched the scene unfold with indifference. He still felt rancor towards Calignac and the madness it had brought him. He could not figure out why everyone kept bringing up this stupid Pilgrims' Path.

Then, before Debasse could make a move, Trouvert took the floor to thank him for placing the needs of the community above all. Indeed, it took a great mayor to put aside ambition to do the right thing for Calignac, Trouvert continued in a commanding and laudatory voice. Raising his glass, the priest made a toast to the man behind the village, the man with a vision, the man capable of extraordinary sacrifices in the name of his community.

And just this morning, Trouvert continued, Debasse had informed him of his decision to go on a pilgrimage to Lourdes in the name of the entire village, Trouvert announced. And this, dear Calignacians, was a remark-able sign of moral leadership in times when others chose the easy way out, the priest finished, turning to Debasse and raising his glass to the exceptional man and his devoted wife, without whom this could never have been achieved.

The priest turned towards the mayor to shake his hand and caught the flicker of anger in Debasse's eyes. The quivering of his lower lip was an indication that the mayor was doing all he could to conceal his utter indig-nation at being used so shamelessly. Once again, the villagers raised their glasses and cheered for Debasse, calling, "Long live our mayor!" several times with joyful enthusiasm. Debasse seemed to lose his footing as he gripped his wife's arm. His world was crumbling before his eyes; everything he had worked so hard to achieve was going up in smoke: all these ambitions and dreams, foiled and thwarted in a flash! He felt trapped in this grotesque circus, surrounded by the broadly smiling faces of the villagers.

Upon hearing the news, Constance's face had lit up with unrestrained pride. As Trouvert often told her, the Lord did work in mysterious ways. Her prayers had finally been answered. Her wayward husband had come to see the light, she mused, cherishing this knowledge.

As the villagers continued to clap effusively, Debasse bowed to the crowd to conceal his embarrassment. He swallowed hard his bitter resentment.

CHAPTER THIRTY-NINE

Dismissing the despicable noisy spectacle, the aloof Courteline turned into a side room where he had noticed a display of glass jars. In each of them, he recognized the familiar outline of floating truffles. He stepped in closer, lost in contemplation. Although he was going back to Paris with a few samples purchased at the fair, he had not made any more progress since his guided tour of Alavert's shop, he thought spitefully. He took a jar in his gloved hand and gazed spellbound at the dark treasures.

He heard a step behind him and turned around to find Mathilde. What a sweet country girl, he thought as he recalled his previous conversation with Adèle. Quietly, Mathilde approached, and they both remained still, captivated by the heavy glass vessels. Courteline pursed his lips; he was trying to find the right words to broach the question that burned in his mind. Without the hope that Mathilde might reveal the secret of the truffles, he would have left this travesty of a feast without hesitation. He had better things to think about—for instance, returning to Paris to manage the confidence crisis that was harming his business.

Weren't truffles amazing? he asked. She nodded candidly. He traveled here far from Paris to see these magnificent specimens in the hope that one day he might be able to make such discoveries himself. He mused aloud, satisfied that the little girl was glancing back at him with curiosity. He could well imagine the thrill experienced at such a moment was comparable to Champollion's after deciphering Egyptian hieroglyphs. He was leaving the day after next and now all hope was lost, he continued in a resigned tone. One could not always get what one desired, he finished, his voice trailing off.

She came closer to him and they both stood in the half-light staring at the jars. *She* had looked for truffles before and obviously with some luck, Mathilde offered earnestly. From an early age, children in the region learned how to locate these underground treasures, she whispered to him as in a promise. In fact, she knew a place where they would surely find some, she proposed as the Parisian tilted his head to the side with genuine interest. She would be going truffle-hunting the next morning, since it was the last opportunity before the season ended, she confided. Would he like to come along? She already had a spot in mind, in the woods where she had seen

Léonard cast wheat seeds. That is where she would take him treasure hunting, she explained.

He was honored to accept her invitation, Courteline responded with poorly contained effusion. An irrepressible wave of exhilaration washed over him. It had been years of knocking on so many doors, but they had all remained closed to him. Now Destiny was putting this incredible last-minute opportunity before him. Everything was lining up so well and in a couple of days, he would be able to take these secrets back to Paris. At last, he was going to experience truffle hunting which no amount of reading or second-hand accounts could surpass. This would be his revenge on this village of madmen, he thought, elated.

Courteline went over to the window and stared out at the starry sky. He was a good judge of human nature, he congratulated himself. He had no doubt that the little girl would lead him to a trove of truffles.

After all, he knew his genius was unmatched.

CHAPTER FORTY

The next morning, staying out of the cold wind, most villagers congregated at the church where Trouvert rejoiced over the reopening of the Pilgrims' Path while others migrated across the town square to Brévin's for an early *apéritif*. The room was teeming with loud chatter and bustle. All of Brévin's usuals were there except for Léonard, who was missing from his usual seat near the window.

Montrelazet and Alavert were sharing a creamy espresso. Hunched over their canes, the elders sat around the heavy cast iron radiators in the back corner. Engrossed in animated discussion, they grumbled with passionate skepticism about the mayor's surprising announcement at Adèle's the night before. At the front counter, Brévin sliced the fresh *tourte* the *Boulangère* had brought over. Nothing like a crusty loaf with butter and cheese! Brévin looked around, amused with the animation the recent news produced. No doubt, the last few months had been filled with many unexpected twists and turns, but last night topped it all!

In the early hours of that same morning, the municipal council gathered as promised, and the Pilgrims' Paths were fully reopened. The re-opening of the paths had left many disconcerted because Debasse's change of mind was uncharacteristic. Most villagers could not understand the whole affair and it bugged them. Was it the result of the mysterious indisposition that had caused him to stay away from the *Fête de la Truffe?* Something was off, they felt; others simply shook their heads in disagreement for they had never believed in the closing in the first place. Was it not plain that Debasse's decision was a direct response to this year's poorer attendance at the *Fête de la Truffe?*

In the back of Brevin's, the elders had yet another opinion on the burning topic. For them, the strange emissions from the fountain had scared Debasse. There was simply no challenging St. Calin, the protector of the village, the elders mumbled as they tsk-tsked, sipped their drinks, and sank their few brittle teeth into thick, delicious slices of bread spread with *cabécou*—Rocamadour's goat cheese—and drizzled with honey.

In the hotel room, Courteline looked around as he packed up the last of his personal effects. The mid-afternoon train would at long last take him back to his Parisian life, away from this mess. He could not wait to return to his cherished lifestyle, replete with luxurious comfort and dazzling sophistication. Despite the recent complications of the news from Paris, his stay in this pit had paid off. He contemplated his reflection in the mirror. Was the skin below his chin sagging? he wondered, disconcerted. He would have his barber massage it upon his return. Now he would drop off his luggage at the station and then head down to Brévin's. He was going to crush these pathetic, unrefined peasants and embarrass them, he thought with jubilation.

Courteline pushed Brévin's door open with resolve and felt all heads turn and eyes focus on him. He recalled them smirking under their breath when he had first arrived a few weeks before. These villagers had no idea what he, the Parisian, had accomplished. Who had the upper hand now? He slid into a seat at the counter and he motioned to Brévin for a plum *eau de vie*. He quickly swallowed it, and as he asked for a refill, he turned to his new audience, generously offering a round to the entire café. They would not forget him, he promised himself. Brévin was only too happy to oblige; after all, this Parisian was a man of means.

So, he was leaving Calignac and heading back to the big city? Brévin inquired as he went about the room, filling everyone's order. Courteline turned to him, oozing with self-confidence. Yes, imagine that—he, a city dweller, had managed to master the trivialities of the countryside in just three weeks. All of Paris would soon know it too, he boasted.

It really took years to truly know things well, Brévin

gently pushed back with his usual joking tone. Several villagers came over and huddled around the counter, drawn by the animated sound of the discussion. They could not pass up a chance to quarrel about the superiority of the countryside over the city!

Courteline motioned to the café owner in a dismissive way. Pfff! Knowing was just a question of *savoir-faire;* he shook his head with haughtiness. *Savoir-faire?* Brévin cajoled, his instincts telling him to press on. Throughout the years, he had seen his fair share of Parisians, and he knew Courteline's type. He leaned forward and poured his pompous customer another drink. This one was on him, he smiled slyly. That would no doubt help loosen up his tongue; big city people were unaccustomed to the strength of the clear spirits that Brévin concocted out of local fruits in his cellar.

Well, what a funny thing fate and *savoir-faire* had brought together, Courteline continued with false modesty. Ah, yes, a revelation indeed, he nodded, his eyes shining with assurance.

Brévin started polishing his bar glasses with his soft cotton kitchen towel. Hmm, a revelation—he did not believe in such things; true revelations came after years of labor, patience, and dedication. They were like truffles, and everyone in the country knew it well, the café owner responded sagely.

Several villagers nodded. Courteline turned around, flattered by the villagers he had attracted and the interest that his presence occasioned. But the truth was that the mere mention of the word "truffle" had sent a flash of hardly contained scorn over Courteline's face. Well, that was precisely what had happened to him, Courteline began. He, the Parisian, had discovered what some spent their entire lives searching for.

Indeed, he had found a truffle, he declared in a long breath filled with feigned modesty.

CHAPTER FORTY-ONE

A thick silence cast a pall over the room. The elders in the back imperceptibly reduced their jabber at the mention of truffles and refocused their old eyes towards this man who stood there in a posture of defiance against their years of wisdom, art, and experience. Villagers stared at each other. Not only had they missed a perfect city-bashing opportunity, but it now looked as if they would have to endure the drivel of this haughty, rotund man while he crowed about the discovery of his truffle. Plus, everyone wondered how this outsider had found what had eluded so many locals.

Feeling the tension build, the Parisian lifted his glass slowly once more. He might as well indulge now; that's something that he could not find in Paris. Brévin chuckled to himself: one shot of his *eau de vie* was enough to inebriate a flock of sheep. So, he knew that they would get to the bottom of this story sooner rather than later. Up on his hackles, Courteline filled his chest like a boisterous rooster. Although a city dweller, he had conquered the rustic secrets of the countryside in a short month. It was merely a matter of studying the trees and the sky, he pontificated, as his fat jaw moved up and down.

Brévin could hardly repress his laughter; the Parisian's physiognomy suddenly seemed grotesque, his foray into the woods ludicrous. But he continued to listen carefully like the other villagers who waited for the meaty details. And as they gawked shamelessly, Courteline gave a detailed account of his search and discovery of the truffle. He recounted the walk through the woods… the golden fly that had helped him identify the location and then his effortless digging…

When he was finished, he drank some more. The alcohol rose and reached the recesses of his brain in a tidal wave. He rested his back against the cool metal bar stool for a second; the strength of this delicious *eau de vie* overwhelmed him.

There was a little brouhaha at the back; the elders were mumbling among themselves before they turned their heads back towards Courteline. They had not missed a word and were rather puzzled and intrigued, to say the least. With his two hands resting on his oak cane, the shortest and most commanding elder craned his neck and summoned the others' attention. From beyond the sea of marble tables, his wise face, weathered by time and hardship, rested intently on Courteline's.

Suddenly, the elder's roguish voice boomed, taunting the Parisian. Ah! *Vraiment*—really! You found a truffle?!

Courteline turned defiantly, his mind blooming with intoxication. What? The elders were challenging *him*? Threatening to topple his moment of glory? He would vie with these dried-up old skeptics and show them his treasure. The air filled with an intimidating tension as the villagers waited, enraptured by this unfurling controversy.

Standing there erect like a farm rooster, Courteline pushed back his shoulders, unnerved by their tone. A smirk on their faces, the elders did not budge as they watched the insufferable man shuffle his portly legs through the maze of chairs. Woods, he said? And where exactly had he found a truffle? Whom had he robbed? they asked in a caustic tone.

The Parisian glanced back at them, quickly understanding the implication. Raising his corpulent hand, he reassured the elders: he had been in the presence of the owner of the field when the discovery happened. The elders nodded. So, it was not stolen. That, at least, was acceptable, they grumbled.

One of the elders extended his hand with authority; the gesture brooked no refusal. Would he not share his glorious find with everyone?

Courteline hesitated, torn between his intent to keep his secret and his insatiable desire for grandeur. He grinned and quickly complied, reaching down into the silky folds of his pocket. He finally produced his treasure. The actual feel of this gem of a truffle had filled his night with exhilaration. He was transfixed by its beauty. The mere sight of it now made his entire being expand and dilate with exultation. The old man motioned him forward and grabbed the truffle expertly between his index and thumb, nodding gravely. He passed it around the table to the other three elders who leaned over it to evaluate the specimen.

The silence was a good sign, Courteline thought, his expectation growing as the minutes ticked away.

CHAPTER FORTY-TWO

Courteline was already reveling in the glowing praise to come. This would be his ultimate triumph. Yet, as the minutes ticked away, he started to feel unnerved at the time they were taking to appraise his jewel. All of a sudden, the elders broke into smiles, their eyes twinkling mischievously. They stared back at him with an intensity that shook him to the core.

His head became heavy, then light. The scene in this tiny village café in the middle of nowhere was surreal. He felt as though he were giving an oral testimony in front of a jury, rather than having an absurd conversation with a bunch of bony, hunched-over old men.

Well, this truffle was a very poor specimen, one elder said; the others nodded in assent.

What did he mean *very poor*? Was it not beautiful? Courteline was bewildered.

It was real but completely worthless, the elder reiterated, sensing that his words failed to register. The texture and scent alone said it all. And in fact, it came from a land that would never be able to produce anything of worth.

How could they be certain? the Parisian asked pleadingly. The elder slowly shifted his eyes again towards Courteline. If he really wanted to know, the diagnosis was actually very simple.

Courteline's face fell as if he had been shot through the heart. Blood drained from his face as he tried to grapple with this impossible verdict that felt like a guillotine coming down on his head. Impossible! They had it all wrong, he thought as his head started spinning out of control. While he tried to regain his footing, the elders remained silent, intentionally leaving Courteline to marinate in a bath of self-doubt.

Where had Courteline found this piece of garbage? the elder questioned. Courteline could not reveal the origin of this find; he had given his word, he swung his head in proud denial, as if clinging to his last ray of hope.

Unfortunately, he had been fooled, the elder pressed on. Any farmer worth his salt would know it was futile to protect a field of desiccated stones that amounted to nothing. The field that produced *this* truffle would never in a million years produce anything remotely worth a centime, the old man added in a suave tone.

As the elders pressed him with more questions,

Courteline felt cornered. But his pride could no longer be silenced.

This was not found in a field, Courteline defended. It was in a vale—a wooded vale, in fact!

What? A wooded vale? *The* wooded vale? Did he really mean Adèle's wooded vale? The elders suddenly merged into harmony in one single voice.

Yes, Adèle's wooded vale, Courteline confirmed—he had been there early yesterday morning with Mathilde. They smiled at each other with mischief, as if they had received the answer to a question they had longed for. Indeed, they had bickered for years about this very topic while they sat around this table, day after day, sipping their coffee and playing chess. No one could believe their ears. The wooded vale had been the stuff of dreams for generations, and when they lay awake at night, they had imagined that this sanctuary held fabulous underground treasures.

Really, Adèle's vale? the elders repeated slowly with almost childish surprise and delight. Everyone knew that, in recent years, acid rain had rendered some fields unproductive. Was that what had happened to the vale? Tight wrinkles formed around the corner of their smiling eyes as they let out mocking chuckles, contagious enough that the entire room quickly echoed their mirthful derision.

Courteline's face turned white as a sheet; was he about to faint or to suffocate? These insufferable ripples of laughter pelted him from all sides. He stood unable to move, paralyzed by the ridicule that fell on him like an unexpected spring rain.

Did you see this? the head elder asked, elbowing his neighbor, pointing at the discredited goods on the table. The wooded vale is sterile and will never yield even a single good truffle worthy of the name! He tapped his index finger on his nose for effect, mockery permeating his whole demeanor.

Limp, Courteline lost his composure, feeling the ground open under him. The rest was a blur. Crestfallen and inebriated, he staggered to the station, clinging to his only remaining salvation: the late afternoon train that would allow him to flee this utter insanity and return to a world that made sense to him.

EPILOGUE

With the warmer spring weather, Montrelazet had resumed his morning walks at dawn well before Calignac awoke. He followed the weaving footpath bordered with oak and giant boxwood trees until he reached the plateau at the top of the cliffs offering breathtaking views of the valley. This air, so pure and uncorrupted, filled him with youthful wonder.

Standing still for a while, he enjoyed the sight of the sun's golden orb when clouds stretched over it like thin wispy strips of wheat. The cheerful black and white swallows squeaked high above him, diving swiftly to gather good. Ah, the power of a pause was prodigious, as Bonne-Maman always loved to say, he mused as he started with renewed energy. Below, the village seemed to breathe softly, small collections of houses with slate roofs and stone walls scattered across the land.

This year had started with big changes for Calignac, he reminisced. After his pilgrimage, Debasse had returned determined more *than ever to win the pending elections. Madame Sardelois had stepped in as the opposition. Although the race had seemed close.*

However, amid all this peace and harmony, one odd and violent incident had taken place in the streets of Calignac. Léonard had swung by the Bouchère to sell her a few wild boar piglets snatched from the woodland. On his way out, puffed up by the profit he had just made, he was hit from the side with such force that for a second, he had flown in the air. His body had landed with a loud thud several meters away and an excruciating pain had ripped his chest open. Everything had gone dark. When he had reopened his eyes, he had been unable to move. Montrelazet had rushed to the scene and found him in a pool of blood, hanging onto life by a thread.

On Léonard's clothing, the Docteur noticed traces of fur-like hair. Then he closely reexamined his patient's wounds in the upper leg region. The impact had been huge, the bruising and bleeding massive, two ribs broken. And on his left hip, a gash consistent with the mark of a canine fang or perhaps a tusk. All the signs had been there: the hair, the position of the wound, the gash—all had pointed to the work of a wild boar, and probably not that of a male—the gash being too shallow.

When Montrelazet looked back, he could not make sense of the incident. What was particularly eerie was that, despite rumors, there had not been a single witness, and, in past decades, wild boars had never ventured into human territory. On that day, however, one enormous beast had apparently stampeded through the village of Calignac. And in a sudden headlong rush, it had settled its score with Léonard. While Montrelazet tried to make sense of the whole turn of events, the villagers were deeply affected by the incident. In their minds, Léonard had gotten his due for killing the sow's farrow. So,

Léonard had met his fate and his cruelty towards Nature had been punished.

Montrelazet was not one to believe in superstitions, yet in some cases such as this one, he was forced to recognize that there was a certain supernatural sense to justice. Furthermore, he could not help but notice that the gory attack had a paradoxically therapeutic effect on the villagers because it validated their instinctive belief in a higher order—this divine justice they so often invoked.

Montrelazet finally reached the front gate of Adèle's house. For months, he had been visiting her every day on his way home. Just checking in, he would say cheerfully, and she pretended to dismiss him with coy playfulness. She preferred not to acknowledge the extent of the pain that kept her captive in bed. Though the visits had been short at first, they had developed into engrossing conversations that lasted hours.

The Docteur had come to look forward to these visits. He found Adèle's nuanced viewpoint a refreshing counterpoint to his highly pragmatic approach to life. That afternoon, he was particularly inclined to share his thoughts.

For his entire existence, he had believed that scientific principles and logic governed all. Yet now, he was starting to wonder... In the past year, it seemed that St. Calin had chosen to protect the village so dear to his heart. There had been signs, heavenly signs, as Trouvert happily put it, events that his rational mind could not explain away as it had always done. Of course, there had been the dramatic discoloration of the fountain, Debasse's rash, and more recently the peculiar circumstances of the mayor's failed re-election, followed by Léonard's most improbable brutal encounter with the wild boar.

In the end, how could one fail to see a connection among all of these events? Was it not fascinating that humans craved order and tended to ascribe meaning and narrative to all events? The Docteur leaned back in the winged chair that had become his designated seat by Adèle's side.

That very morning for instance, he went on, as if to make his point, he had awakened from an unusual dream in which an owl had landed on his windowsill just after a letter from a long-lost friend was delivered. A few hours later, there was a knock at the door, and the mailman had brought a letter from this very friend, announcing his imminent visit to the region. Strangely enough, on his way to see Adèle, he had heard the unmistakable cry of that same nocturnal bird from his dream. Was it that his mind was more receptive because it had been sharpened by the dream?

Now, it had become impossible for him to accept that such a series of uncanny events could have occurred randomly. There had to be an improbable force springing on these events.

He made a dramatic click of the tongue, as if to prompt her reaction. He knew that Adèle indulged his inspired musings with the mocking benevolence of a sister, both encouraging and derisive at the same time. He paused for a minute, noticing the lines that deepened around her eyes. She gazed at him, and he took her elegant hand that had grown so pale. He squeezed it gently; he would miss her thoughtful presence, he thought, drawing a breath as a feeling of sadness overwhelmed him.

Maybe, rather than acknowledging mystery, his entire pragmatic vision of the world—his refusal to accept ambiguity—had been his primary blind spot? He felt forced to seriously consider that possibility... It was what some villagers called destiny or fate, this unwavering force that connects apparently random events by a string, as if *guided by an invisible hand. He knew that although she often teased him about succumbing to such irrational thoughts, Adèle agreed that this invisible hand guided their steps through their daily choices. It was a matter of responding to the calls that life threw at them with the highest degree of moral integrity in action and conduct; that was the meaning of life. Surrendering to this knowledge was an act of radical acceptance and, perhaps, the ultimate achievement.*

HE KNEW she smiled at the turn of events that had shaken the village and the changes they had produced throughout the community. He knew that she marveled at her granddaughter's budding love for the earth. It was all she had ever hoped for. He noticed the serene acceptance of her silence. He gazed at her, as if reading the thoughts that flowed across her brow like clouds breaking for a short instant in a summer mackerel sky.

SHE WAS READY.

AFTERWORD

From passing away to passing down, there's only a snap of the fingers, a fraction of a second. At that moment, those who stay behind get reminded of the phenomenal power of life.

But why is it we sometimes feel we are sleepwalking through it all?

When I was diagnosed with cancer, a feeling of overwhelming urgency took root in my heart and soul. It felt as if another biological clock had kicked in.

I started realizing I had put too much attention on existing rather than living. These days, there is an inordinate amount of pressure on young people to find their way, their "purpose in life." It's time we flipped this paradigm on its head, and, in equal measure, let purpose find us. This is not a passive question—on the contrary—but a balanced one between reciprocal assertiveness and shared contemplativeness.

It's far from easy. While I have sought comfort in the arduous writing of this novella, it has taken me 20 years to do so!

Fortunately, along the way, I re-discovered painting. Painting empowers me to even greater heights. I especially love the shorter distance between artistic expression and the emotional exchange I get from my visitors and collectors.

A twinkle in your eyes, a smile on your face, deep inhale. With energy, dedication and discipline, I would argue, you are ready. Start with the generous and jovial exploration of your emotions, passions, and roots.

ON THE ART OF CONTEMPLATION

As Bonne-Maman says, *"The power of a pause is prodigious."*

Contemplation has tremendously helped me quieten my mind, cultivate awareness, and live more fully.

If, like me, you are eager to find greater presence, clarity and—ultimately—connectedness, visit me and my paintings at cecileganne.com—to find out more about the guided art contemplation workshops I have been running.

Curious about the world behind *Scent of a Truffle?*

From medieval villages perched on limestone cliffs to bustling markets filled with black truffles, *duck confits*, saffron, and rich Cahors wine, the *Lot* region invites you to slow down and savor life's simple, exquisite pleasures.

Scan the QR code below to uncover a curated page featuring beloved destinations, time-honored recipes, trusted sources for French culinary treasures, and glimpses into the rich cultural heritage that inspired *Scent of a Truffle.*

ABOUT THE AUTHOR

CÉCILE GANNE grew up in southwestern France in the Dordogne Valley, a beautiful region nestled between the prehistoric Lascaux caves and Rocamadour, a sacred pilgrimage site on the Way of St. James.

She now splits her time between her art studio in Boston and Wellesley College, where she teaches French language and literature. When not painting, Cécile enjoys traveling, swimming, and walking in nature.

Her artwork can be found at Cecileganne.com.